THE PETROVA BETRAYAL

A SCOTT STILETTO THRILLER 4

BRIAN DRAKE

WOLFPACK
PUBLISHING
— EST 2013 —

The Petrova Betrayal

Print Edition
Copyright © 2019 (as revised) Brian Drake

Wolfpack Publishing
6032 Wheat Penny Avenue
Las Vegas, NV 89122

wolfpackpublishing.com

Print ISBN: 978-1-64119-638-3
Ebook ISBN: 978-1-64119-637-6

THE PETROVA BETRAYAL

CHAPTER 1

Somewhere in Iraq

THE LEFT TIRES almost lifted off the pavement and the right tires screeched terribly as Hardball wrenched the Jeep around a tight corner, the two men in the back holding tight to whatever grip they could find.

Scott Stiletto, his knees on the hard metal floor of the back seat, felt the wind rip at the collar of his partially-open khaki shirt as he raised his AK-47 and eased back the trigger. Flame licked from the muzzle, his salvo aimed at one of the two trucks in pursuit. Return fire bit at the Jeep, and he clenched his jaw tight. None of his rounds appeared to have hit.

From behind the wheel, Hardball shouted, "Almost there!"

"Can't this heap go faster?" Stiletto asked, straining to shout over the whine of the stressed motor.

Hardball did not respond. The bald mercenary, so nicknamed because the top of his head resembled the rounded tip of a full-metal-jacketed bullet, kept low with his hands tight on the wheel. The street wasn't helping, large cracks and bomb craters creating hazards equal to the automatic weapons fire behind. The wreckage of blasted buildings flashed by on either side, and any people in their way scattered. What struck Stiletto were their frightened faces. They were not fighters, but innocents caught in a war not of their own making, trying desperately to survive amongst the constant threat of stray bullets. And that made him mad. Stiletto fired again, the AK bucking against his shoulder. The windshield of the truck closest to the Jeep spider-webbed and shattered, and several rounds connected with the gunners in the passenger and rear seats. The resulting chunks of flesh and the blood splashing the cabin did not appear to distract the driver. Stiletto shifted his aim, the Jeep jolting on the rough pavement, and squeezed off another salvo. The driver's head snapped back, and the truck veered off the road and smashed into a light pole.

One truck left.

Return fire zipped overhead, but Stiletto didn't hear it so much as feel the small shockwave of each bullet. Something chunked into the back seat, tearing open the vinyl, stuffing flying into Stiletto's face as he dropped the empty mag and shoved another into place.

Beside him, Short Fuse took over firing, his AK-47 spitting rounds and the hot brass landing on Stiletto's back. Short Fuse was as good with a rifle or a pistol as he was with a bomb.

Stiletto had hired both to help him with an assassination mission from the Israelis, the target a Palestinian mastermind training insurgents in Iraq. The whole plan had gone belly up quickly, and now they were on the run—and the target still breathed.

Stiletto shifted out of Short Fuse's muzzle blast, trying to fire as the Jeep took another sharp turn—to the left this time, the tires screaming again. He would have complained except that turn meant the landing zone was only a few blocks away.

Both AK-47s spat flame and their rounds struck the hood of the pursuing truck, whose gunmen were leaning out the windows to fire back. Stiletto tried to target one of those gunners, but his shots went wide when the Jeep hit another bump. He aimed instead for the front tires, shouting for Short Fuse to do the same. Presently one of the front tires popped and the truck swerved wildly left and right, causing the gunners to become more interested in hanging on than fighting. Short Fuse faced forward, Stiletto continuing to cover their rear, as Hardball kept the accelerator floored.

Stiletto looked ahead. The bombed-out warehouse they'd used as a hideout grew in the distance, and Stiletto was very happy to see the exposed steel beams where walls had once been. Almost there, indeed. He looked skyward, but there was no sign of the pickup chopper.

Stiletto stayed low and hauled a satellite phone from under his shirt. "Where are you?"

"Ten minutes out," replied the pilot, his voice almost crystal clear over the handset.

"Copy. We're at the extraction point."

Hardball brought the Jeep to a stop near the open front of the warehouse and the trio hopped out, dragging equipment bags with them. The pursuing gunners had no vehicle, but they still had feet. Four of them ran toward them.

"Inside and to the roof," Stiletto ordered. Hardball and Short Fuse double-timed into the building and pounded up three flights of steel stairs to the roof.

Most of the roof remained intact. The chopper couldn't land, but the pilot planned to get low enough for the team to climb aboard via a rope ladder. Now that they were exposed and on the run, their clandestine escape would be anything but.

Hopefully, this time luck was smiling on them.

Stiletto reminded himself that he didn't believe in luck. The only things that would get them out of this were skill and the ability to plan on the fly.

In the event of an attack, Stiletto and his men had arranged piles of concrete in various places throughout the warehouse and on the roof to use as cover. They ran to those spots now, Stiletto and Hardball choosing locations close to the roof's edge while Short Fuse found a spot covering the stairwell opening they had passed through.

Stiletto jammed a fresh magazine into his AK-47 as he took in the area around him. A lot of the city was rebuilding, but most of the structures remained damaged, crumbling from lack of attention and continued fighting.

"There they are," Hardball called, and Stiletto looked down at the street. The four surviving gunners from the second truck were spreading out on either side of the street.

"What are they waiting for?" Stiletto wondered.

The wind picked up, cooling the sweat on Stiletto's neck. The breeze carried with it a distant rumble.

Hardball cursed.

A block away, an armored truck with a cannon on the roof turned the corner.

Hardball said, "Twenty-millimeter, by the looks of it."

"They'll knock this building down like a house of cards."

"It's a good day to die," Hardball replied. The sky was clear, the sun burned bright, and the empty desert in the far distance looked majestic.

But Scott Stiletto had no intention of going to the hereafter this day.

"You can die here if you want," Stiletto told him, rising and heading for the stairwell. He yelled for Short Fuse to follow. The stocky bomb expert didn't argue, and followed closely on Stiletto's heels.

They were halfway down the stairwell when the twenty-millimeter cannon launched its first shell. The building shook violently, the explosion shredding what remained of an upper wall and sending chunks of concrete and other debris flying everywhere. Stiletto stumbled and fell down the stairs and crashed to the ground, the hard metal tearing his clothes and cutting open exposed skin. The stock of the AK-47 slammed hard into his belly as he fell. Short Fuse grabbed the railing to remain upright. Gasping hard, Stiletto fought to rise. He couldn't hear, everything hurt, and bloody patches now dotted his clothes from top to bottom. Through gaps in the wall ahead, he saw smoke curling from the muzzle of the cannon and the four troops primed for an assault.

Something tugged on his shoulder—Short Fuse. He mouthed something about having a plan and Stiletto nodded. He had a plan too: hit them from behind and get a bomb on the back of the armored machine, if they could survive to get close enough.

His hearing started to clear, but the shrill ringing persisted. Gunfire crackled from above.

Hardball. The shell hadn't taken him out, and his shots peppered the ground near the assault troops, driving them to cover. Stiletto and Short Fuse charged through the front of the warehouse and headed for an alley across the street. One of the troopers saw them and let off a burst that kicked up chunks of asphalt. Short Fuse reached the alley first, sliding a pack full of explosives off his back. As Stiletto reached the corner, shards of brick and dust exploded in his face, gunfire zipping past him to smack the wall of the alley ahead. Stiletto pressed his back to the corner of the wall, swung around, and jerked the trigger to unleash the full magazine on the trooper in pursuit. The slugs spread across the man's chest, opening body cavities he'd hadn't been born with that spilled his guts all over the ground.

Short Fuse was halfway down the alley, and Stiletto ran after him as he reloaded. The cannon boomed again, and there was another explosion. Stiletto hoped Hardball was out of the way, and a short burst of return fire answered his question. *Keep 'em pinned, buddy. We're almost there.* His face stung from the brick shards as he and Short Fuse reached the opposite end of the alley.

They turned right at the exit, stopping at the

building's corner. Up the street sat the armored truck and the troopers, and Stiletto pointed at the troopers closest to them—the ones on the right side of the street—and drew a finger across his neck. Short Fuse nodded, opened his bag, and took out a wrapped satchel charge, pulling out a fuse cord. He ran for the cannon, and Stiletto braced himself against the wall.

After the twenty-millimeter roared again, another section of the warehouse wall crumbled and a plume of dust stretched through the streets. The AK bucked against Stiletto's shoulder as he aimed at the two troopers, shifting his aim with each burst. One trooper's head exploded like a melon and pelted his partner with gore. Before the second could turn, he joined his dead partner in a bloody heap on the street, the red stuff mixing with the dust and turning it to reddish mud.

Short Fuse slapped the satchel charge to the armored truck, the bomb's magnets holding it in place, then turned and started running back. As Stiletto covered him with the AK, a winking muzzle flash on the roof of the warehouse proved Hardball still lived. Short Fuse reached the corner and he and Stiletto hit the ground as the explosion filled the street, more dust and debris taking flight and landing around them.

Calm settled on the combat zone. If there were police or military units on the way, Stiletto couldn't hear them, the cannon fire and bomb explosion leaving him temporarily deaf except for the ringing in both ears. He looked up. There was no sign of the chopper either. He reached for his sat phone, but it wasn't in his pocket where he'd left it. It must have fallen out somewhere along the way. Where was the chopper? Had more than ten minutes gone by?

Stiletto pushed to his feet, gestured for Short Fuse to follow, and they ran, unsteadily at first, back the way they had come and returned to the smoking warehouse. The steps were gone, so the only way up was a ladder they had rigged at the rear of the building. The rungs extended through a hole in the roof, but it had fallen over during the assault, the hole in the roof being a little bigger now. Short Fuse put the ladder in place again while Stiletto covered their backsides, and the explosives expert started up, the ladder's uneven legs causing it to rock a little with each of his heavy steps. Stiletto climbed after him.

Once on the roof, they found a dusty Hardball

still behind one of their makeshift cover spots, his face and head cut a little.

"That was close," he said, although Stiletto only heard a little of it. Short Fuse pointed east, and the helicopter appeared over the top of neighboring buildings. It was a fine sight to see. *We might live to fight another day after all.* The chopper hovered over the roof, and the cabin crew dropped a rope ladder. The team started climbing, leaving their gear behind. Stiletto entered the cabin last and fell across the metal floor. He was gasping, bruised, and bloody, but alive. He could deal with the failure of the mission later. The chopper dipped its nose and turned south.

CHAPTER 2

Tel Aviv, Israel

THE NEXT DAY Stiletto stepped out of an elevator and onto the rooftop pool deck of the Isrotel Tower in Tel Aviv. The pool sat at the very top of the tower, and might as well have been isolated in a desert. The sounds from the city below couldn't reach them, so he heard nothing but laughter and splashing.

At the bar, he ordered a Maker's Mark and Coke. Moving to the blue rail surrounding the edge of the roof, his body aching in mild protest, he leaned against it and gazed out at the clear blue Mediterranean in the distance. The frolicking continued behind him, providing an interesting soundtrack to his introspection. The color of the water matched the sky, and the warm temperature felt good. The view seemed very peaceful, but that water had witnessed a lot of bloodshed that had no end in sight.

The city below went about its business silently, while up on the pool deck, a carefree attitude ruled the day. Stiletto turned to face the pool, which was occupied mostly by kids. Watchful parents remained on the sidelines, while a trio of young ladies sunned themselves on loungers. Each one wore a bikini to show off their flawless bodies, as well as sunglasses, and had an automatic rifle lying next to them. Stiletto shook his head. IDF troops on a break. The endless war was never far away.

He sipped his drink with a glance toward the elevator. No sign of his Mossad contact yet.

His team had left Iraq and returned to the back room of the downtown Tel Aviv bar where the failed operation had been assembled. Very quickly they broke down their gear and went their separate ways, but not without Stiletto trying to get them to agree to continue the mission.

Both had refused. They'd been paid to go into Iraq and assassinate a target. The failure of said mission left them with no obligation to chase the target unless Stiletto was willing to fork over more cash.

For Stiletto, that was quite a letdown. To him, the job wasn't done until the target was dead.

He didn't know anything more about Jafar el-Gad than his Mossad contact had told him. Apparently the man was a PLO captain and the brains behind a variety of attacks incorporating new killing techniques. El-Gad didn't do any killing with his own hands, but he showed others how to do it and sent them into battle. Mossad wanted him dead, and Stiletto had hoped to deliver. It was his first major free-lance assignment since being sacked from the Central Intelligence Agency, and it had gone from a smoothly executed plan developed in a Tel Aviv bar to a pile of rubbish in a Baghdad street.

His life since leaving the Agency had been hectic, chasing after every dollar to keep the hounds at bay. Since most mercenary activity went on in Europe, he'd had to relocate from his home in Virginia to an apartment in Paris. It had not been an easy transition. Most of the work he'd scrounged, such as guarding North Sea oil rigs, involved long stretches of tedium and being on the water, which he hated, but his checks always cleared.

His life was in a state of disruption, but not for the first time. He'd adjust.

He drank some of the Maker's and Coke, and the elevator doors slid open. Asaf Cohen, Stiletto's Mossad contact, stepped out and took in the sights before him; his head moved left and right and lingering a little too long on the bikini-clad IDF sunbathers. Stiletto whistled and Cohen snapped his attention to him, grinned, and approached with an easy gait.

"Good morning," Cohen said, shaking hands with Stiletto. "What are we drinking?"

"Maker's and Coke."

"This early?"

"It's after midnight in the States."

Cohen took a deep breath. Stiletto couldn't see his eyes behind the dark aviator glasses, but he sensed those eyes were looking right at him.

"What did you want to see me about? Your job is done. Go home."

"The job is incomplete," Stiletto corrected.

"Missions fail all the time. We knew the risks when we hired you. If you had been killed—"

"I know, I know. You didn't want it traced back

to Mossad. I get that. But I also have my pride to think about."

Cohen laughed. "Pride will get you killed."

"My reputation?"

Cohen shrugged. "I suppose it's not good to be known as somebody who can't finish his tasks."

"You paid me a lot of money."

"You needed to pay your men. By the way, where did they go?"

Stiletto shrugged. "Who knows? I tried to get them to stay with me and keep going, but they refused. They were paid to go into Iraq, and they went there."

Cohen shook his head with half a grin on his face. "You have a lot to learn about mercenaries, Stiletto."

"Or how to find men with a better work ethic."

"That has nothing to do with it. Mercenaries are the way they are, and that's why we hire them. No fuss, no drama. *You're* creating drama by trying to be a hero."

"I'm simply trying to earn my money."

"You earned it. Go home. We'll catch el-Gad another day. You know how it is. Miss him on Tuesday, get him on Friday."

"Today is Friday."

"You know what I mean."

Stiletto folded his arms. "What if I want to kill el-Gad on principle?"

"Because he needs killing?"

"People like him, yeah. So these people," Stiletto gestured toward the pool, "don't have to worry about somebody blowing up this hotel."

Cohen removed his sunglasses and squinted at Stiletto. "I'm going to tell you this as a friend," he said. "Don't get too deeply involved in things. You need to stay detached."

"The CIA used to tell me the same thing."

"That's what got you fired."

"You'll note that I took the consequences and moved on with my life."

"What happens if I tell you Mossad will not sanction continued action?"

Stiletto waited for a beat, and then said, "I'll do it on my own. Worst case, I end up dead. The *worst* worst case, I end up guarding oil rigs again to save more money."

"Those oil rig jobs are quite unpleasant." Cohen put his sunglasses back on. "When was the last time you visited Greece?"

"That's classified."

Cohen laughed again. "Ah, spies. Tell you

what, go somewhere away from here and do some serious thinking. You might like Athens and a casino called Regency Mont Parnes. Lots of good play, lots of attractive women. Like those over there."

"You probably know them."

Cohen took the opportunity to glance at the three women over the top of his aviators. "Nope. Not those."

Stiletto said, "How long should I think about things?"

Cohen shrugged. "Couple of days. I'm sure the answers you're looking for will come to you quite quickly. Be seeing you."

Stiletto watched Cohen leave. He didn't look like a veteran of various secret campaigns carried out in defense of his country.

But then, Stiletto didn't look like a killer either.

And Stiletto had a real talent for taking out bad guys.

Stiletto waited a few more minutes to give Cohen time to get to the lobby and back to his car and away. He leaned his elbows on the railing and gazed out at the Mediterranean.

Of course, he took missions personally. Well, some of them. It was a flaw, and his bosses at the

Agency had pointed that out many times. But there were some who deserved a champion—somebody who could fight the battles they could not—and Stiletto considered himself that champion. It was thankless and crazy, yeah, but when one has the power to make a difference, one should exercise that power. Responsibly. Carefully. Devastatingly.

He needed a victory over el-Gad for another reason. Everything felt upside-down, inside-out, out of control, and he needed to reverse the situation, to feel less like a car speeding off a cliff. He'd felt the same when his wife died.

Stiletto and Maddy had married young and struggled greatly during the early years of Stiletto's military service. Their daughter Felicia had added further complications, but they were a happy family for a while despite Scott's constant travel for the Special Operations missions that took him away from home for weeks at a time. He had finally retired at the rank of major and had been all set to take a cushy security job in New York City when Maddy had died of cancer. After that, Felicia decided she didn't want anything to do with her father and took off on her own. Scott had no idea why his daughter hated him. She had never explained, and his mind often spun in circles trying to discern the reason.

His latest situation wasn't as bad as losing his family, and he could at least cope with the changes.

But it was still hard.

The Med offered no comment. Only the ocean and the land lasted forever. Everything around him would someday be gone, just like the civilization that had preceded this one had faded into history. What would it look like then? From that perspective, Stiletto wondered what the point was. Why risk his neck when history would eventually forget he existed, and the only witnesses—the ocean and the land, forever presiding over human folly—couldn't talk? Then he realized he was thinking way too much.

There was a splash behind him, and somebody screamed. Stiletto turned to look. Some knucklehead had cannonballed into the water and the splash had made a direct hit on the bikini-clad IDF women, who were now laughing it off as they dried themselves. One was shooting a nasty look at the fellow as he swam past lazily, pleased with himself.

Stiletto returned to his hotel room on the eighteenth floor. Using his laptop, he booked a flight to Greece.

.   .   .

THE CABLE CAR swayed as it traveled upward above the slope of the mountain below, which was a carpet of dark green. The treetops looked bristly from above, and very unforgiving should the cable car somehow fall through the forest canopy to the ground. Stiletto had to admit it was a nice view, though. Behind them, the lights of the city blazed against a curtain of black. Ahead were more lights, but isolated in a single spot. The lights of the Regency Casino Mont Parnes were almost as bright as the city lights, but not as dazzling.

Stiletto loved Greece, especially the coastal areas, and had once spent a week's vacation at a seaside resort, but he hadn't been back in several years despite his quip to Cohen. This trip, and the reasons for it, made the venture less enjoyable than if he'd been on holiday, but if he could finish what Mossad had hired him to do, he might change his tune.

There were two ways to get to the Regency. The first was to follow Parnithos Road that wound around the mountain, twisting and turning its way through the forest and requiring special attention, especially at night. There were no lights on the road, and a driver who was tired, slightly inebriated, or simply not paying attention, faced disaster should he or she run off the road or overcorrect on one of the hairpin turns.

The other way, and the more popular, was the cable car, which started at a station far down the mountain outside Acharnes, a suburb of the greater Athens area. The cable cars were always packed, and Stiletto stood against the Plexiglass window with a crush of other Regency guests behind him. Standing room only. The parking lot at the cable car station had been full when he arrived by taxi, so that meant anybody taking their own car would have to brave the road.

Stiletto had been visiting the casino every night for the last three, tracking Jafar el-Gad, his girlfriend, and his two-man security entourage. Asaf Cohen's suggestion of finding the Palestinian at the casino had been so spot-on that Stiletto knew they'd been tracking the target even before Stiletto had made his plea to continue the mission. He didn't fault the Mossad man. A lot of things in the spy business happened based on suggestions, hints, and creative interpretations of other men's words. It was up to people like Stiletto to make sure they made correct assessments of such indirect instructions.

Sometimes it was enough to make a guy crazy. Why couldn't they say things directly, like normal people? That, Stiletto thought with a short laugh, assumed that spies were indeed normal people. He seriously doubted they were.

As the cable car continued to creep along, the voices of the people surrounding him slightly muting the groans and whines of the thick cables holding the cabin aloft, Stiletto ran through what he knew about el-Gad.

El-Gad and his crew visited nightly for a round of poker that often ended in el-Gad losing money. They avoided the cable car. El-Gad's bodyguards drove him around in a four-door Jaguar XJ, white in color, and the reason was obvious: the cable car represented a cage in which el-Gad could be trapped. Stiletto would have made the same call, except that tonight he needed the cable car. He'd left his own car near the exit in the casino parking lot, and planned to follow the Palestinian back to his hideout in Athens. Their use of the road meant Stiletto could, if he made the effort, find an ambush point and blast the Jag off the road, but that would endanger civilians also using that route. If he were still with the CIA, they could do a drone strike as the car traveled, but he no longer had that option. He was on his own. He had to solve the inevitable problems that always came up in such a way that required nothing more than his ingenuity. He could do it, but he wished he didn't have to. He wished he had help. He wished a lot of things.

He let out a sigh that created a small patch of condensation on the Plexiglass. The cable car was almost to the top. Stiletto wanted to be there *now*.

The cable car finally docked at the receiving platform, and Stiletto waited while the other passengers disembarked into the dazzling and brightly lighted casino. He heard a lot of Greek, a few foreign languages, and some English. The Regency catered to tourists and locals alike.

Stiletto made his way through a floor covered with buzzing and dinging slot machines, weaving around clusters of people trying to navigate their way through the massive area, and presently exited the front of the casino into the parking lot. His shoes scraped the outside steps and tapped a rhythm on the blacktop. It looked like every parking spot had a car in it, bright lamps lighting the way. His rented BMW sat in the farthest corner. Stiletto dropped behind the wheel and let out a deep breath. He couldn't see the white Jaguar from where he sat, but there was only one exit, and he'd see the car for sure when el-Gad and his people departed.

Now he had to stay awake and not get bored. The soft leather seat felt like a couch. He turned on the car's accessory power and rolled down the windows to let the cold air in, then turned on the radio and found some music to listen to. Lastly, he removed a Montecristo cigar from the inside pocket of his jacket and struck a match. If he had to sit and wait, he could at least enjoy himself.

Two-hours later he'd finished the cigar and tossed the butt out the window, his mind numbed from watching every single car that exited the parking lot. Plenty of white cars, but no white Jaguar XJs. He began to wonder if el-Gad had broken his nightly routine for the first time, but then he finally saw the four-door Jag making its way down an aisle. Stiletto pressed the starter and buckled his seatbelt.

The BMW's powerful V8 burbled as he joined a short line of leaving cars, luckily none of them white. The mountain road was one lane each way, so there was no chance of losing the Jag or of getting ahead of them. They, too, had the disadvantage of having other cars in front of theirs. Once they reached the streets at the bottom of the mountain, where a four-way intersection allowed many different options for travel, he'd have to hustle to keep up.

The road was twistier than Stiletto thought, but the BMW handled the cornering fine. The centipede of cars, with their flashing brake-lights and headlamps, lit the roadway enough to give him plenty of time to react to the curves. Speeds remained moderate, and of course, the white Jag XJ remained three cars ahead. The forest on either side looked dense.

After a half-hour of twists and turns, they cleared the mountain and reached Meg. Alexandrou, Stiletto staying close to the Jag as other vehicles branched off in different directions. They drove by homes and more trees. There were trees everywhere, separating the homes or lining the streets, as if the builders hadn't the heart to cut down all of them to make room for the houses. When they reached Orfeos Road, the houses became more spread out, then fewer and fewer, and Scott drifted back to put more space between him and the Jag. They were back in a wooded area, with street lamps to light the way. Other cars passed in the opposite lane, so being on the same road as el-Gad and his crew would not immediately be suspicious. Had Stiletto been in the other car, he'd have his senses on high alert anyway.

The Jag slowed, brake lights flaring, and Stiletto took his foot off the accelerator to slow down a little as well. The Jag made a sharp left turn and Stiletto kept going, glancing at the rear of the Jag as he passed, noting the long driveway up to another house secured behind the wooded roadway. Stiletto continued up the road another mile and pulled over with the engine still running. On his iPhone, he noted their location and coordinates. He could get a better look at the place on his laptop back at the hotel. He waited for two cars going the opposite way to pass before swinging the BMW in a wide U-turn and heading back the way he'd come.

CHAPTER 3

HE FOUND the house via Google Maps, his HD screen giving him a very sharp overhead picture. The news, however, didn't get any better.

The computer rested on his lap as he sat on the hotel room's small leather couch, which had no back support, so sitting on it for any length of time made his lower back ache. But it was a smoking room, so while he puffed on another Montecristo, he examined the photo. Large house with what looked like a red-tiled roof, a lot of overgrowth in front, and a crescent driveway that connected at a single point with the access road from the street. A closer zoom revealed a chain-link fence blocking the property off from the wooded area surrounding it, and there were no other structures close by.

Plenty of places to hide, yeah, but for him *and* the enemy. Was the fence electrified? What kind of security did the house have? Cameras, certainly. He set the machine on the seat beside him and pondered the lit end of the Montecristo. He could do some digging and learn what kind of security measures had been installed, who owned the place, and other ancillary details, but that wouldn't change the fact that if he tried to take out el-Gad while he was home, he'd have to go it alone.

He'd done that sort of thing before, but there had always been backup standing by if the situation went south.

He didn't have that advantage any longer.

The option remained to give up on this crusade, but instead, he found himself more determined than ever to see it through. And then the tactical side of his mind took over and started formulating a plan. He typed a list of needed items and grabbed his phone. There was only one person to call for the gear he required, and the man answered right away.

"Yes?" The man spoke guardedly, his voice low.

"Liam, it's Scott Stiletto."

The voice brightened. "What can I do for you?"

Liam Miller ran one of the biggest arms-smuggling operations in Europe, and he also worked as a CIA informant, an arrangement Miller found useful for getting rid of competitors. He wasn't as big a snake as some of the criminal informants on the Agency payroll, however.

"I need some things. I'm paying cash."

"There are a lot of rumors going around about you. Any of them true?"

"Probably. Especially the one about me having been fired from the Company."

"That's the big one."

"Yes, it's true. That's why I need to buy some gear."

"I'll give you the friends-and-family discount. What do you need?"

Stiletto read from his list, having to repeat an item once or twice. Miller occasionally suggested that he might have to replace a named item with a similar equivalent, but Stiletto didn't mind as long as the substitute performed well.

"What about ammo for your pistol?"

"Yeah, I need some of that too."

"Still the forty-five?"

"Of course." Stiletto's pet pistol was a Colt Combat Government. He'd added a match-grade barrel for better accuracy, glow-in-the-dark night sights, and had some fine-tuning performed on the action for better reliability.

"Where are you right now?" Miller asked.

"Athens." Stiletto told him the name of his hotel.

"I'll be there personally in forty-eight hours."

Stiletto ended the call. He'd need to have the cash transferred, but there would be plenty of time for that.

He'd also have some time to scout the target a little and answer some of his questions about what he might face when the shooting started.

JAFAR EL-GAD DROPPED ice cubes into two glasses and poured brandy over the ice.

He crossed the wide living room to the couch where Miska Mooda sat with her long legs crossed and one arm on the back of the couch. She watched him with sleepy eyes and accepted one of the glasses.

"I'm getting tired of the casino, Jafar," she said.

He eased onto the couch next to her, and the

leather cushion hissed under his weight. The room was well-appointed and clean, but lifeless. Nobody lived here regularly. The house was there specifically for people like him who needed to be missing from normal operating areas for a period of time. The carpet was thick, the beds were soft, and he didn't mind if his superiors wanted him "missing" for a lot longer.

"I need to win back my money," he said.

She laughed and swallowed some brandy. "You'll never win your money back. You're a lousy poker player."

He frowned, then shrugged. "You're probably right."

"One more night," she said, "and then we find something else to do."

"It's safe there."

"It's safe all over here," Miska said.

He looked past her at nothing.

"What's wrong?"

"They got close."

"But we beat them."

"We didn't kill them."

"It was typical Mossad," she said. "They'll go try to kill somebody else now. You're off the list for a while."

"You want to get back to the fight."

"I'm bored. How much longer?"

"I check in day after tomorrow. We'll see what the boss says."

"Tell him *your* boss says we need to go home." She grinned. They'd met during an operation in Iraq, where the PLO sent several teams to target US forces in what the leadership called "live training exercises." El-Gad led the teams, his men perfecting some of the bomb-making techniques he'd developed. He and Miska had a lot in common, including the loss of family due to Israeli missile attacks on PLO strongholds.

"How would my boss like to spend the rest of the evening, remembering that our two guards are also in the house?"

"Well," she said, setting the glass on the coffee table in front of them and crawling across the couch to him. Her spaghetti-strap top fell open a little.

"I think I'd like to place a bet."

Her heat enveloped him. He met her gaze without blinking.

"What kind of bet?"

"Take a guess."

He did.

. . .

STILETTO WATCHED the house the next night, lying flat in the forest about fifty yards away. He was close enough to observe without needing binoculars.

The guards didn't patrol the area. They stayed inside, maybe walking around the house now and then. El-Gad and the Mooda woman mostly remained in the house as well. They didn't all leave until evening, and Stiletto knew their destination was, once again, the casino. His mind started modifying his plan. If he could be in position the next night when he had the gear Miller was bringing, he could take out the car and everybody in it and not break a sweat.

Miller arrived the next afternoon with his trunk full of the requested items: a black combat suit, matching boots and face paint and an M-4 carbine with an M-203 grenade launcher attached under the barrel that could fire high-explosive, buckshot, or gas shells. Miller brought some of each, but Stiletto wished he'd brought more of the high-explosive. Ammunition for the Colt .45 and night vision goggles rounded out the kit. He paid Miller and set about inspecting the gear and trying on the boots.

The following night, loaded for bear and

blending with the forest shadows, Stiletto watched the house and cursed.

El-Gad and his crew didn't appear to be going anywhere.

One of the guards took the car and was gone for about forty minutes, returning with two bags of takeaway food. El-Gad must have become tired of losing at poker, and now Stiletto had to shift back to his original plan. He changed positions, moving to a hiding spot twenty-five yards behind the house. He watched them through the rear windows, which allowed a view of the kitchen and part of the dining room. They all sat at the table and dished out the food, el-Gad and one guard visible. Miska Mooda and the other guard were out of sight. Stiletto fed a high-explosive round into the M-203 and tucked the rifle stock into his shoulder.

He flicked the selector switch to full-auto and tightened his index finger on the trigger. The M-4 spat flame, the low recoil barely registering, the muzzle rising only a little. The salvo shattered the back window, creating an opening for the high-explosive projectile. Stiletto moved his trigger finger to the M-203, and the charge launched with a thump and a harder kick. Stiletto watched the grenade sail through the open window. The occupants were already reacting, somebody letting out a yell as the shell continued through the dining room and passed through into the next room. Stiletto cursed as the explosion rocked the house, a ball of flame consuming the other room and blasting chunks of wall into the dining room. He bolted from cover, banging his head on a low branch, and ran for the fence, easily vaulting over and landing on the soft grass opposite. Somebody was at the window firing single shots, the rounds splitting the air around Stiletto and smacking into the grass. He fired the M-4 on the run and the gunman dropped for cover.

Stiletto blasted the patio door and ducked through, feeling part of his blacksuit tear on a sharp piece of glass still in the doorframe. He pivoted right and fired into the kitchen, and the gunman hiding on the floor rocked with the hits and sprayed blood over the countertop. El-Gad fired from around the corner and Stiletto blazed back, tearing chunks out of the wall. El-Gad didn't fall. Stiletto dropped the empty mag and slammed in another as he advanced, carefully crossing the kitchen floor and firing blindly into the dining room. He saw two bodies on the floor, the other guard and the woman, their corpses ripped open from the high-explosive blast. El-Gad grunted, letting out a cry of pain as Stiletto moved around the first guard he had shot and stepped into the dining room.

A jagged piece of wood stuck out of el-Gad's back—part of the table. Pain strained the man's face as he lay on the floor, but he still had enough strength to raise a pistol with a shaking hand. Stiletto calmly sent a burst through his chest that ripped open his upper body and a single shot into the head. El-Gad flopped as the slugs tore through and moved no more, what remained of him half-propped against the blood-spattered wall.

Stiletto's boots sank with a squish into the wet carpet as he went around the table to check the other bodies, but neither the guard nor woman moved. He exited the room and retreated the way he'd arrived, his pulse racing, mind now fixed on a getaway that promised to be much easier than what he'd faced in Iraq.

NOBODY in the crowded airport terminal paid attention to Stiletto as he sat waiting for his boarding call, his carry-on suitcase with the x-ray-proof bottom at his feet.

He sat quietly drinking a Coca-Cola and thinking about the mission.

It had gone well. Better than expected, and he had enough money left from the Mossad contract to take time to consider his next job. No more guarding oil rigs for the time being.

Mossad was happy, Asaf Cohen having called while Stiletto checked out of the hotel to say they were pleased to call the mission a success. Stiletto wanted to know how Cohen already knew, because he hadn't told them. Cohen only laughed. The wonders of Mossad, he'd said.

For a job he had accomplished in order to make himself feel better, it was a bust.

Scott didn't feel any better at all.

A sense of accomplishment, yes. It was nice to be able to say he'd completed the task he'd been hired to do, albeit with unexpected delays.

He still felt lost, and again told himself it would take time.

But how much time?

Stiletto's cell rang, and he removed it from his pocket.

"Yes?"

"It's Suzi. Where are you?"

One of Stiletto's first moves upon moving to

Paris had been to contact Suzi Weber, a former CIA analyst. She was confined to a wheelchair after almost getting killed in Iraq, but maintained her contacts in the intelligence and underground communities as a support specialist and coordinator for freelancers like Stiletto. Clients called her to get to him, leaving Stiletto free to move about as needed and avoid direct contact with clients until a meeting became necessary. He paid her a commission with each job.

"Airport waiting for my flight."

"If you want some more work, change your ticket to Seattle."

"Why?"

"A defense firm has a problem, and your name came up as somebody who might be able to solve it."

"Tell me more," Stiletto said with a smile.

Seattle, Washington

THE WAITER LIT the candle in the center of the table. Harry Ames gave the man a weak smile and watched the flame flicker, then dropped his eyes to the glass of bourbon, where the flame's reflection shimmered. He took a long drink, the alcohol burning his throat as it went down.

Ames sat at a corner table near the entrance, his jacket still on to guard against the cold chill that rushed in every time a new customer arrived. The bar was dim, and the flash of exterior street lamps that lit the backs of new arrivals provided his first glimpse of those who came in, especially the women.

When he wasn't casting an eye at the ladies, the television above the bar with football on the screen held his attention. The sound was off and the bar was filled with low music, nothing that particularly stood out to Ames.

The door opened, and the cold air tickled his neck. He swallowed more bourbon. The woman who entered looked great, wearing a dark blouse and slacks that hugged her shapely rear end, but the examination ended when he saw the man with her, his hand on her back, his gold wedding ring flashing before the door swung shut.

Ames looked into his drink.

Couples were always tough.

They reminded him of his dead wife.

The waiter passed the table, and Ames ordered a refill, finishing what remained in his glass before the waiter brought the next. Ames raised the glass to his lips but then set it down. Making a mess of himself wasn't going to bring Connie back. It also wasn't going to help him "get back out there," as his colleagues kept saying. He wasn't sure what that meant, but he wanted to report that he'd at least tried. Maybe that would start to make him feel better. Or maybe he should adjust to being alone and maintain the relationships with close friends that he'd built up over the years. He didn't have to be "alone," per se.

He wondered what Connie would think as he swallowed some more of the bourbon.

THE DARK-HAIRED WOMAN at the corner table opposite Harry Ames had been watching him for over an hour. He apparently hadn't noticed her, since he gave his attention to every woman who walked in and none to those who were already seated.

Darien Foster nursed a glass of white wine while planning her approach. She knew all about Harry Ames, his past and current situation, and thought she knew how to exploit his weakness.

Because it *was* a weakness. If he hadn't had

Dead Wife Syndrome, she'd have found another. She was an expert at such things and very rarely guessed wrong.

Darien and her team couldn't have picked a better target. Harry Ames was the Chief Engineer on a top secret project at the Jordan Corporation, a defense firm with an exclusive Pentagon contract. They were working on a next-generation radar system that could detect stealth aircraft. All very gee-whiz hush-hush stuff, but the system had the potential to alter modern warfare. Many other nations would pay, or even kill, for a chance to possess the plans.

They'd investigated several Jordan Corp. employees looking for the right person to exploit, and Harry Ames topped the list.

There were other ways to accomplish their goal if the plan failed, but that only made Darien laugh. She was dressed to kill in a tight red strapless cocktail dress that hugged every curve of her petite athletic body and left nothing to the imagination. If Ames didn't do a double-take when he finally noticed her, the man was made of ice.

She waited for Ames to order his third drink. When the waiter brought the bourbon, she slithered out of the chair, took her glass by the stem, and crossed the floor to his table.

She stopped less than a foot from the chair opposite Ames and smiled. When Ames looked up, his eyes resembled those of a sad puppy. The man was a mess, but he didn't look away. She saw a flash of desire behind those sad eyes and opened with a simple line.

"May I join you?"

HARRY AMES' throat suddenly felt dry.

He took a deep breath and said, "By all means," then watched the slender fingers of her free hand pull out the other chair before she slowly dropped onto the seat. When she leaned forward, the top of the dress showed a deep valley, and something stirred inside Harry—a mix of excitement, desire, and nervousness. What was she doing here, talking to him? She was young. She was beautiful. She could have her pick of the litter. Why him?

"I figured," she began, "that two people alone in a bar should probably introduce themselves."

"I'm Harry."

"Darien."

"Are you new in town?" he asked. It seemed

like a decent question to start with. Maybe she wanted somebody safe to talk to while she watched for somebody more interesting.

"Been here a few weeks, actually. Just started a new job with one of the local tech firms. I write code."

Harry nodded. He knew a little about the IT world, but only a little. He told her so, adding, "Mostly I only call the computer people when my machine crashes."

Darien let out a laugh. "That's most of our day, for sure."

Harry hid a frown. She certainly wasn't like any IT person working at Jordan, but heck, she was a pretty girl and he was there to meet somebody, so why not make the most of the opportunity?

They talked about living in the city. Seattle was a crowded place. Everybody complained about the lack of parking, and Darien was no different. She told Harry how she often left her car in the garage under her apartment building and walked or took Uber everywhere. When she discovered that she was actually saving her money that way, she realized it was a plus rather than a minus. She liked driving up to the Sky View Observatory and getting lost in the wonder of the city, so she had no desire to get rid of the car yet. Wasn't much of a car, either, just a little Chevy she'd had for ten years.

They talked about the museums and libraries and agreed they didn't like clubs or loud bars, and that the bar they were in was one of the quieter ones where you could sit and enjoy your drink and actually hear the person you were with.

Harry loosened up after a while, making a joke now and then and laughing when she laughed. He couldn't believe how much they had in common. For a chance meeting, it was a fortuitous one.

CHAPTER 4

DARIEN FINISHED her wine and Harry ordered her another. He was finally relaxed, and his eyes had gone from sad to eager. Almost too eager, which was fine. She had him right where she wanted him.

The dolt had no idea that he'd been watched for the "couple of weeks" she'd been in town, and she'd made it a point to note every place he frequented. Their commonality was a carefully-prepared scam.

After an hour, with his fourth bourbon almost gone, Harry excused himself to use the restroom. "This stuff runs through me like water," he said, and she laughed again.

"The perils of too much of a good thing," she replied.

He laughed again and left the table. Darien looked around. Nobody was paying any attention to her. She lifted her left leg, reached into her shoe —she was wearing the three-inch heels tonight— and pulled out a small glass vial that opened with one twist. She poured the contents into Harry's glass, and the clear liquid vanished in the pale amber of the bourbon.

When Harry returned a few minutes later, she raised her glass. "To a great conversation."

"A wonderful conversation," he said, clinking glasses with her. They downed what remained of their drinks.

Harry leaned close. "How about you come back to my place? I have some twenty-year-old scotch I think you'll find delightful."

"I can't imagine a better way to continue the evening," she agreed.

HARRY HOPED she didn't notice that his hands were shaking as he started to pull out her chair.

The tavern door opened, letting in another blast of cold air that touched Harry's cheek just right. He looked up at the two women walking in, both in the middle of a conversation, and the blonde in the dark suit made him freeze. Too much hairspray had made a helmet of her hair, and it stopped right below her ears like his wife's had. She too had always used too much hairspray. The woman passed him, and Darien turned to look at Harry.

"Are you going to let me out?"

"What?"

"I need more room to get up, Harry," she said, forcing a laugh.

"I'm sorry," he said, bolting for the door before it swung shut. He hurried along the sidewalk, breathing hard, and stopped near a lamppost. He leaned against it, catching his breath.

"Hey!"

Darien rushed toward him. "What's this about?"

"The blonde who came in. She looked like my wife. I can't go home with you. I'm sorry."

"Harry—"

"Please. I can't."

He kept his eyes on the sidewalk. His breathing had slowed, but she still stood there. He sensed her eyes on him, but he didn't look up. If he looked at her, he'd lose his resolve. This could not happen tonight, and maybe not any night. Maybe he should stay a widower.

"Well, it was nice talking with you, Harry," Darien said, hurt in her voice. "Have a good life."

Harry mumbled something, and she finally turned and walked away. Her heels tapped on the sidewalk for a long time, and then he couldn't hear her anymore.

Harry Ames swallowed and hailed a passing cab. Climbing into the back seat, he gave the driver his address. He blinked a few times as his eyes adjusted to the darkened interior with its odd smell and the mesh screen between him and the driver. When he put a hand out, he could barely see his fingers.

Then everything went black.

Darien sat in her car a few blocks from the bar and dialed a number on her cell.

"Is he ready?" a male voice said.

"Forget it," she said. "I almost had him, but he got cold feet. I couldn't wait for him to pass out. He got a cab and probably passed out in that."

"Find him."

"How? Once the cab driver sees him out cold, he'll either dump him on the street or take him to a hospital."

"This is not what we planned, Darien."

The woman laughed. "No kidding, Sherlock. We're going to need a Plan B."

"Plan B was to hit him over the head and control the situation."

"We can call it Plan C then, but we need to start working now because we're running out of time."

She heard the man breathing on the other end and waited. While she waited, she examined one of her fingernails. Getting a little rough around the edge, she thought. She looked at the others. Might as well do them all, she decided.

"We'll talk about it tomorrow," the man on the other end of the line finally said.

"Good night, sweetie."

Before the man could reply, she ended the call and started her car. Paying the booth attendant, she merged into traffic and the slow-moving parade of cars.

STILETTO LANDED at Seattle-Tacoma Airport with

no fanfare or prior announcement. After getting his passport stamped, he rode down an escalator to the baggage claim area, getting a sense of the sprawling complex. High ceilings, a lot of windows, and model airplanes dangling from above greeted him as he stepped off the escalator. The flood of people on the shiny tiled floor completed the picture of a major metropolitan airport.

Airports were all similar to him. He had no favorites, but there were a lot he disliked for their size and difficulty in navigating. SeaTac had one oddity, though, that was seldom found. It was such a large airport that they required an underground light rail system to move passengers from one side of the airport to the other. It was particularly annoying when trying to make connecting flights. Stiletto knew first-hand about that and the noise it generated in the narrow underground tunnel. He'd once been forced to use the light rail or miss a connecting flight back to Fort Bragg during his army days. His CO at the time would not have been pleased had he called to say he'd be late in reporting back.

He moved with the flood for a moment, then stopped and stepped out of the travel path. One of the airplanes hanging from the tall ceiling was the

Rutan Voyager, a replica of the record-setting airplane that had flown around the world without stopping for gas. Stiletto had been ten years old when Dick Rutan and Jeana Yaeger had made their flight. His father, an Army man with a strong interest in aviation, had watched the live take-off and landing as if both were the football games he tried never to miss. It hadn't made much of an impact on Stiletto at the time, but it made one now. The plane represented somebody with a dream who gave it all to see that dream come true. Stiletto had had a dream once—to serve his country and the people in it, and to have a family of his own— but that dream was now over. As he stood gazing at the long wings and the tube fuselage that was tapered at either end, he knew he'd have to find another dream.

And that was okay. Change wasn't easy, and his new life seemed like a daunting challenge, but Stiletto was game for the effort.

Stiletto reached the baggage carousel and collected his two suitcases. The clothes within were dirty. His first priority, after getting squared away with the new client, was to run everything through a laundromat. He laughed to himself. He might as well have been a college kid again.

A man in a black chauffeur's uniform waited near one of the exit doors, holding a sign with his name on it. Stiletto approached the man and identified himself. The driver insisted on seeing his identification, which Stiletto provided, and then tucked the sign under one arm and grabbed the suitcases. Stiletto followed the man out to the parking lot, where they presently reached a black limousine.

Gray clouds above and a hint of moisture in the air. It wouldn't have been Seattle without the threat of rain, Stiletto decided. The driver loaded the suitcases while Stiletto settled into the plush interior. Well, he could sure get used to traveling like this! He stretched out his legs while keeping his carry-on close to his side. That was one piece of luggage he didn't want to leave his sight.

No liquor lined either side of the cabin, though the shelving for such was there. He did see an assortment of soda pop and water, along with snacks. As the driver sped away from the airport terminal, he announced over a small speaker that it would be about a forty-five-minute drive to the office since traffic was heavy, so Stiletto helped himself to a Coke and a bag of almonds.

The passing scenery meant little to Stiletto as

it flashed by the tinted windows. At a stoplight, a pair of kids in the back of their mother's car waved even though they had no clue who sat behind the darkened glass. Stiletto waved back anyway.

Downtown consisted of more heavy traffic and steel-and-glass office buildings, various shops, street vendors hocking food or other items, and an eclectic mix of professionals and free spirits. On one corner, a man sat in front of a trio of over-turned buckets and played them like drums, banging out a catchy rhythm.

When the limousine turned into a private garage beneath one of the tall buildings, the outside noises ceased. It was a small garage, mostly concrete and very chilly. The driver joined Stiletto in the elevator, escorting him to the security guard in the lobby, who picked up a desk phone and placed a call to somebody named Mr. Campbell. Stiletto tipped the driver, who then excused himself, promising Stiletto that his luggage would be waiting for him in his hotel room. Stiletto looked around the lobby. The tiled floor sparkled, and the front of the building was mostly glass. A small plaza extended from the front doors to the street and several people in suits milled about, either talking on cell phones or smoking in a corner away from the rest.

The security guard, a young man in his twenties, was shorter than Stiletto, and he seemed uncomfortable in his suit. He hung up the phone and told Stiletto that Mr. Campbell would be down in a moment. The kid sat behind the desk and started flicking switches on a pair of monitors in front of him. Stiletto remained where he was.

The elevator dinged, and the doors rumbled open. A man taller than Stiletto stepped out and approached. His custom-tailored suit fit him well.

"Mr. Stiletto?"

"That's me."

They shook hands.

"I'm Elias Campbell. Thanks for coming. Ms. Jordan is expecting us in her office."

Campbell had a full head of blond hair and might have been one of those few individuals who are continuously carded at bars because of their youthful appearance. However, his height communicated clearly that he was no perpetual twenty-year-old.

As the elevator doors slid shut, Campbell pressed a button for the twentieth floor and stood with his hands behind his back. He made no eye contact with Stiletto, instead pointing his gaze at the top of the elevator car, so Stiletto made no attempt to engage him. Everything he needed to know would be said in the presence of Kim Jordan, the CEO.

Suzi had given him a rundown on Jordan. Mid-thirties, single, inherited the company from her late father. Jordan Defense was known for pioneering new technology that was almost always adopted by the military, but details were few because the tech was still classified. Stiletto had seen plenty of new gizmos while in the service; gear he was allowed to use and teach others to use, but they weren't allowed to ask any questions about where it came from. It had probably come from places like Jordan Defense.

The elevator stopped suddenly, and the doors slid open on a large private office. Between the elevator and the desk at the far end were a sitting area and a conference table, the furniture resting on plush carpeting. The wood-paneled walls weren't faux. It looked like they had been hand-carved from freshly cut trees. Campbell led Stiletto across the floor to the desk. A woman sat behind it, her back to a row of windows looking out on the city and the threatening gray clouds.

The woman rose when Stiletto and Campbell came within six feet of the desk. She was shorter than Campbell (Stiletto figured everybody in the building was shorter than Campbell) and wearing a no-nonsense business suit that also announced she was a lady. She had long brown hair, a small nose, and sharp brown eyes that sized Stiletto up as he stopped before her. Stiletto didn't avert his gaze, and she didn't blink.

"Ms. Jordan, this is Scott Stiletto."

Her face relaxed, and she smiled. Stiletto returned the smile, said hello, and shook her hand. She gestured to the chairs in front of her desk. Stiletto and Campbell sat. The chairs surprised Stiletto. They weren't set lower, the way most CEOs did to give them the appearance of looking down at their guests. The chairs' seats matched the level of Kim Jordan's. They were all on eye-level with each other.

Except for Campbell, of course. Damn genetics.

"What do you know about my company, Mr. Stiletto?"

"Secret Pentagon work, lots of classified stuff. You keep secrets very well. I'm an Army veteran and a former intelligence officer, and I can't say

I've ever come across your company's name before."

Kim Jordan smiled. "You're right. We like to keep everything here a secret, even the number of paperclips in the storage room. But somebody is trying to steal our secrets, and we need that to stop."

"Tell me more."

"To give you the whole story means I have to share some specifics of what we're doing." She opened a drawer and took out a piece of paper. "Are you willing to sign a waiver saying you'll not divulge anything you hear in this office?"

"Of course."

She slid the paper across the desk and handed Stiletto a pen, and he scribbled his name on the bottom. He pushed it back to her.

"Jordan Defense," she said, "is currently working on new radar technology that can detect stealth aircraft."

Stiletto whistled.

"Does that impress you?"

"Very much. But as far as I know, only the United States has a stealth aircraft inventory."

"Other nations are pursuing stealth technology, which was bound to happen once we perfected it."

"And this radar system will give us an advantage—unless the enemy gets their hands on it first."

"Correct. The Chinese and the Russians are already doing something similar. We need to have it before they do."

"Do you suspect your problem is tied to China or Russia?"

"I'm not sure who's behind it. A few days ago, there was a major hacking attempt on our systems, but our firewalls blocked it. Then last night, they made a move on one of my engineers." She lifted her telephone receiver and spoke to someone she called Harry. She asked him to join her in the office.

Kim Jordan made small talk with Stiletto while they waited. Campbell sat quietly. She asked Scott about his background, and he provided answers. She didn't ask about the CIA or why he wasn't there anymore. Either she didn't know he had been fired or didn't care. She struck Stiletto as somebody who was only concerned about having the right people do a job, and not necessarily concerned with how they completed the task. She continued sizing up Stiletto as he sat there. He wondered what she was thinking.

The elevator opened again and an older man

entered, his hair streaked with gray. He walked with his shoulders down. Something bad had happened to him, and he hadn't yet recovered his confidence. Stiletto, Campbell, and Kim Jordan rose as the man reached the desk, and Campbell brought over a spare chair. Kim Jordan introduced Harry Ames, and they all sat.

"Harry, tell Mr. Stiletto what happened."

Harry Ames took a deep breath, swallowed, and cast a nervous glance at Stiletto.

He told his story from beginning to end, leaving nothing out. Stiletto admired the man for being so brutally honest about what must have been embarrassing as well as hurtful.

"You woke up in the hospital?" Stiletto said.

"The cab driver brought me to the emergency room, yes," Ames said. "My speech was slurred. I had a hard time breathing. Two orderlies had to haul me out of the car like a side of beef. The doctor said I'd ingested Rohypnol."

"The date-rape drug?"

"The same," Ames said.

Stiletto turned to Kim Jordan. "This crew isn't kidding around."

She nodded.

"Are you sure this woman," Stiletto said, "intended to steal something from you?"

"It was my first thought," Ames said. "I had just come from the office. My security card is in my wallet."

Kim Jordan added, "We've been on alert for a few months now. Ever since—"

"The hacking?"

"And a break-in at my home."

"Anything taken?"

"No. They spent all their time in my home office. Luckily I had nothing related to the company stored there."

"File a police report?"

"No."

"Why not?"

"We don't want the government involved, Mr. Stiletto," she said. "If they think there's a problem, they'll shut our project down, and my company will go under. Without the military contracts, we can't keep the doors open. That was why I called for outside help. You come highly recommended."

"Because?"

"I know all about what happened with you and the CIA, Mr. Stiletto," she explained.

"Really? Your sources are very good."

"The best. You're the man I want for this job. You'll have access to the entire building and all of my employees. Whatever you need to get to the bottom of this."

Harry Ames offered, "I can describe the woman for you."

"That won't help much," Stiletto told him. "I can't very well go searching for one person. Not in a city this size, and she was most likely wearing a disguise, a wig or something." He pulled a small notebook from his inside jacket pocket and Kim Jordan handed him a pen.

"Let's hear what she looks like anyway," Stiletto said, scribbling notes. When Ames finished, Stiletto turned to Kim Jordan. "I'd like to talk to any of your staff who might be targeted like Mr. Ames was."

Ames sank a little in his chair.

"It's okay, Harry," Kim Jordan assured him. "You didn't do anything wrong."

Ames nodded.

"You'll have our full cooperation," she said. "If anybody gives you a problem, see me."

"Okay."

Campbell rose from his chair, tugging his blazer to straighten it.

"Elias will take you to your hotel," Kim Jordan continued. She grinned at the tall man.

Stiletto stood. "I hope I can solve your problem."

"We didn't talk about money," Kim Jordan said.

"Oh, don't worry," Stiletto said. "If I don't solve the problem, I won't charge you."

"That's—"

"Crazy, I know. Roll with it."

Kim Jordan smiled, and Stiletto smiled back. He followed Campbell and Harry Ames back into the elevator.

As the elevator car descended, Harry Ames let out a breath. "I'll never speak to another woman again."

Campbell laughed. "Oh, Harry."

"Can't blame him," Stiletto said. "But look at it this way, Harry. They thought you were enough of a big shot to target you first, but you were too smart for them."

"What do you mean?"

"Did you really excuse yourself because of your wife, or did you, deep down, think something was wrong?"

Harry Ames furrowed his brow. His mouth started to open, but Stiletto cut him off.

"Don't answer me," Stiletto said. "You can keep that to yourself."

Harry Ames nodded, and his shoulders straightened a little.

CHAPTER 5

STILETTO YAWNED in the back of the limousine.

Campbell said, "Jetlag is a killer."

"You'd think I'd be used to it," Stiletto replied.

It was the only exchange the two shared as the driver made his way downtown to The Paramount Hotel on Pine Street, an eleven-story building sandwiched between larger buildings in a busy section of town. Stiletto's spirits lifted a little. It was small, probably very quiet, and something independently run instead of a chain. He liked it immediately.

Campbell shook Stiletto's hand, and promised to call in the morning, after breakfast, and pick up Stiletto for a tour of the Jordan Defense offices.

Stiletto watched the man get back in the limo

and drive away, then entered the lobby. Soft carpet, lots of wood paneling, and low lighting—a very rustic look. It reminded Stiletto of the kind of no-frills den his grandfather had built at his ranch house in Montana.

The room on the third-floor impressed Stiletto as well. As promised, his luggage sat on the king bed. The room included a work table and a small couch in front of a flat-screen television. He turned on the lights and opened the window to let the cool outside air filter in.

His stomach growled, so he ordered a sand-wich from room service and sat down on the small couch. It felt like sitting on a cloud and didn't make his back hurt. Stiletto dozed off, only to jerk awake when he heard a sharp knock on the door.

He ate by the window as another wave of tired-ness swept over him. If he slept through too much of the day, he wouldn't get any rest tonight, so he left the hotel and started walking to check out the surrounding streets and familiarize himself with any potential trouble spots. He laughed when he mostly saw coffee shops, used clothing stores, and other examples of quiet civilian life. This was Seat-tle, not Iraq.

He bought a cup of tea at one of the coffee

shops and sat by the window with a sense that he was a nobody locked in a cage, watching the world go by.

Maybe that was what he was now. Instead of feeling sorry for himself, he once again resolved to hang in there. He'd adjust and feel better.

KIM JORDAN PULLED her Mercedes into the garage and hit the button to close the automatic door. It shut with finality, sealing her off from the outside.

The house was dark except for the stove light she left on in the kitchen, which provided enough illumination for her to see a light switch as she entered. The kitchen was spotless, as was the rest of the single-level multi-million-dollar home. She had a cleaning crew tidy the place once a week but had to admit they often didn't have much to do. She lived in her bedroom and the TV room and the kitchen. All the other rooms remained empty and unused, their doors closed. This wasn't *her* house, as she'd told Stiletto. It was her father's house, and she'd taken over the home like she'd taken over the company after his passing.

She poured a glass of wine and leaned against

the kitchen counter, staring at a rumbling refrigerator that had no decorations and not much inside, either. She was exhausted and didn't feel like eating anyway.

She thought about Scott Stiletto and the job she had assigned him. He had to work out, because otherwise she'd be forced to call the FBI and have the feds handle the investigation, which would effectively shut down her company. The Pentagon would pull their contracts and security clearance if they knew there was a leak, especially if the stealth radar detection system fell into enemy hands.

Kim Jordan wasn't so much concerned about herself in the matter. She had Daddy's money to fall back on. But she *was* concerned about preserving his reputation. She was chasing his dream, she knew, not her dream, but that didn't matter because she didn't have one.

She'd graduated from UW's College of Engineering and quickly found work at various defense firms, where her father's gentle nudge here and there helped her get through the door. She'd excelled at mechanical design and robotic systems management, but only because she didn't know what else to do with herself. She might as well learn the family business. She had no clue about what to do with her life, and that had affected every decision she'd made since.

Jordan Defense provided nice things, like her car, and her wardrobe, whatever else she wanted, but the house was empty and dark. A clock in the family room ticked, the only sound in the home other than her breathing.

She shook her head. If Stiletto stopped whoever wanted the stealth radar detection system, she simply had to take some time off and figure out who she was.

Kim Jordan swallowed the rest of her wine and walked down the hall to her bedroom.

The purring cell phone woke him up.

Stiletto, still dressed, lay on the bed with the nightstand light blazing. The *Motor Trend* he'd picked up on his walk was on the floor.

So much for staying awake.

He tapped the Samsung and put it to his ear.

"Hi, Suzi."

"Did I wake you?"

"Yeah." Stiletto looked out the window. The sky was dark, and the clock on the nightstand read ten p.m. "Jet lag sucks."

"So does the description you sent me," she said. "How do you expect me to match this to anybody?"

"Somebody with your ingenuity should be able to make something of it."

"You have no distinguishing features. Nothing that makes her stand out from one million other women on the planet."

"Not even the name Darien?"

"It's not common, I'll admit, but it also doesn't help unless this woman has a criminal record somewhere, and if she's part of a group that's involved with industrial espionage, you can bet she'll use an alias. Or maybe you're new around here?"

Stiletto groaned. For all of her attributes, Suzi could be a real pain in the neck.

"Are you telling me you're not going to help?"

"Not with this tiny amount of info. I need more."

"Fine. Okay. I'll get more. Maybe. Probably."

"Go back to bed."

The line clicked, and he switched off the phone's ringer. Rolling off the mattress, he trudged into the bathroom to clean his teeth and jump in the shower before crawling back into bed, sans clothing this time, and dozing off once again. He might wake up earlier than the roosters, but at least he had a chance to get back on track.

"I THOUGHT you could use something strong this morning," Kim Jordan said.

Stiletto almost told her he wasn't a coffee drinker when she brought over a steaming mug of English Breakfast.

"Nothing in it, right?" she asked.

"Correct." Stiletto took the mug.

He sat in front of her desk holding the mug in both hands. The steam drifted toward his face. She sat at the desk with her coffee, some Ethiopian blend she rattled on about for five minutes as Stiletto sat and nodded. He understood the enthusiasm coffee drinkers expressed for their beverage of choice. It was the same enthusiasm he brought to cars and cigars, but he didn't bore people with every little detail of how the Dominican Montecristo #2 was rolled and what leaf it was rolled with and why those leaves made it special or discuss the attributes of the '68 Camaro's rear Positraction.

Because most people didn't care.

Stiletto frowned as she finished. For a moment,

her eyes left him and she vanished into herself. He wondered what was really on her mind.

When she switched to business, she made full eye contact again and seemed to have regained the resolve he had noticed in their first meeting.

"Before we do the office tour," she said, "I should get you up to speed on the basics of what we're doing. What do you know about radar?"

"Other than it makes little blips show up on a screen that tell you how far away an enemy is, not much."

"Basic radar works," she said, "when radio waves transmitted from a fixed station bounce off a target, say an airplane or ship. Those radio waves bounce off steel and metal like stray baseballs."

Stiletto nodded.

"Stealth fighters, and incidentally, stealth ships —yes, we're working on those too, imagine a stealth aircraft carrier—deflect those same radio waves so they don't show up as blips on anything."

"They can't be totally invisible, right?" Stiletto said. "Something shows up."

"Using low-frequency radar, yes. But LF can't detect stealth with accuracy. If you're in the Iraqi desert and you see an indication that something might be coming your way, you can get the anti-aircraft guns and the missiles warmed up, but you won't have enough information for a target lock. You still won't be able to launch until the bomber is right on top of you, and by then it's too late."

"Fascinating."

"It really is. I've been immersed in it most of my life."

"Now tell me about the new radar that can make stealth obsolete."

She laughed. "Did I say that yesterday?"

"It was the impression I got."

"Well, it's not entirely true, although some want to think that's the case. What we're working on here is called 'quantum radar.' Do you know what that means?"

Stiletto covered a grin with a sip of tea. "Hardly my major in college, Ms. Jordan."

"Please call me Kim," she requested.

"Okay."

"I'll make this as simple as I can, because you can really get bogged down in the details and if you don't know the basic science, it's easy to get lost."

Stiletto frowned. Was she calling him stupid?

"What we're experimenting with is using entangled photons sent out by fiber couplers that will bounce off a target, stealth or not, and give us a signature. We'll get the position of the object, its relative speed and direction—all the things conventional radar can give us."

"Enough information for a target lock?"

"Exactly."

"By the way," Stiletto asked, "what the hell is an entangled photon?"

"Well, I can give you an extract from the Bohr-Einstein debates. It's all there."

"You're playing with me, Ms. Jordan." He smiled. He figured she was testing him despite saying she'd make it simple. She couldn't help but *not* make it simple. It wasn't a simple subject. Somebody like him, with no background or education in the science involved, had to accept that the described concept either worked in the real world or it didn't. For all he knew, it was just theory, and in testing, Kim Jordan's little "quantum radar" toy would produce nothing of the desired results.

She smiled back; the sides of her nose crinkled when she smiled. "Photons are all around us. They're particles of light. What quantum radar does is focus and enhance those particles, like a laser, but nothing like you've seen in *Star Wars*."

"Always preferred *Star Trek* myself," Stiletto told her.

"Entangled photons mean those particles are joined together—two become one, that sort of thing —and they stay together no matter where they're directed."

"Now I get it." He raised his mug in a mock toast and laughed. "Do you have a working prototype or a design?"

"A design, lab tests, and computer models. Nothing's been built yet."

"Where is your lab? That might be a target."

"The location is classified, and it's not in Seattle or the State of Washington. Only I and two others on my staff know where it is. And the people who work there, of course."

"What you're building can't be anything new," Stiletto said, "if Einstein has a footprint on it."

"Einstein has a footprint on everything," Kim said. "The Chinese and the Russians have been working on this too. That's why we're racing to get ours done first. The US has had the advantage of stealth technology almost exclusively for decades. If either the Russians are Chinese are developing their own stealth fleet, we need to be able to see it. You know, just in case."

"I'm well aware of those scenarios," Stiletto replied.

"I suppose you would be, wouldn't you?"

"Part of the old job, yeah."

"The thing is," she continued, "we aren't sure either of them has it or that they've made the advances they claim they have. China says they finished the project, but nobody's seen any evidence of it."

"My old department wouldn't have been concerned with it either, so I'm no help."

"You wouldn't tell me anyway, Mr. Stiletto."

"Call me Scott."

"Am I right?"

"Yes. We keep secrets like that for a reason."

"But the government thinks it's a strong possibility because it's a high-priority project."

"They've given you a lot of money, haven't they?"

"A *ton* of money."

"And somebody, you think, is trying to steal your design. Which lends credence to your idea that one or the other of the opposition doesn't have it."

"All I know is what we're paid to do. The government trusted my father with jobs like this, and they trust me by default. I need to deliver, and at least need to make sure nobody steals our work."

"That's what I'm here for. How about a tour of the facility so I can find my way around?"

That smile again. "You read my mind."

THEY LEFT the office to tour the building, Kim taking Stiletto through mazes of cubicles to corner offices where she introduced him to each department head. The upper floors were set aside for research and testing, with clean rooms prominent. Stiletto didn't think his investigation would require interaction with everybody he shook hands with, but it didn't hurt to be known.

After the tour, Kim took Stiletto to a neighboring coffee shop. She found a table by the window. Stiletto shifted in his chair. Coffee for Kim, another one of those fancy blends. He chose green tea with a slice of lemon.

"I like sitting by the window," she said. "People-watching is fun."

Stiletto said nothing, but as she raised her cup, he noticed she wasn't wearing a wedding ring.

"Do you watch other people because you wish you were in a different place?" he said.

"I like Seattle."

"That's not what I mean."

"I know what you mean. Is it obvious?"

"Only because I know what it's like."

"How do you deal with it?"

Stiletto blinked. The question surprised him.

"I mean," she clarified, "how do you not feel stuck?"

"I don't know," Stiletto mused. "It's especially tough now because I'm going through a huge change. I'm focusing on work."

But the question required an attempt at an answer. Maybe later.

"We suspect the Russians or Chinese," she said, regaining her in-control demeanor, "but how would they go about it? What's your guess?"

"Freelancers, for sure—the kind with a specialty with industrial espionage."

"Can there be a lot of suspects, then?"

"Depends. When I get back to the hotel, I'll make a few calls and see what rumors are flying around. Somebody's always talking."

She dropped her eyes again.

"Hey."

When she looked up, her eyes seemed sad.

"When you decide to make a change, you'll make a change."

"Is it that simple?"

Stiletto shrugged. "It's a rumor I heard somewhere."

Once they were back at her office, Kim excused herself and Stiletto took the opportunity to check in with Suzi.

"Anything more on that description?" she asked.

"Forget that for now. I have another idea."

"Okay."

"See if you can find any trace of a hijack crew that might have come to Seattle. Focus on any groups known to work for the Russians or Chinese."

"I'll get back to you."

Stiletto hung up and stood at the window, looking at the thick gray clouds and the steel-and-concrete landscape. The top of the Space Needle stood out near a skyscraper. When Kim returned, Stiletto suggested they get lunch there. She hesitated for a moment but then agreed. Stiletto needed her to loosen up a little. Challenges lay ahead that Kim Jordan needed to be ready for.

CHAPTER 6

"WHAT ARE YOUR PLANS?"

Darien Foster tried to keep the edge out of her voice as she spoke into the phone. She sat in her car near the rear entrance to the Golden Willow casino.

"I'm late for a meeting now," she said. "I'll have a better idea when we're done."

"We are running out of time," the man on the other end said.

"It's not your fight," she said. "Let me worry about the timing."

"It may not be my fight, but it's my money you're burning."

"Gotta go."

"Don't you—"

Darien killed the connection before she could be told what not to do. Exiting the car, she crossed the parking lot to the back entrance and went inside. There was no neon in the rear of the building, just parking lot lamp stands, which was a blessed relief after the barrage of colored light on the street.

A lit hallway greeted her, the offices on either side locked and empty. One door said Accounting and another Operations, but she never spent time with those people.

The hallway ended at a closed door and she went through to one of the main gaming rooms, mostly slot machines and other electronic amusements. She wove through the crowd, who appeared not only oblivious to her but each other. The flashing lights and clickety-clack of the machines were more vivid than anything else.

A short elevator ride took her up two floors to a private conference room where three men waited. They all looked at her as she approached the large table in the center of the room.

"You're late," said the man standing at the head of the table.

Darien dropped into a chair. She didn't respond.

The man, Royal Saunders, glared at her. He owned and operated the Golden Willow. To Darien, he was a necessary tool for what she needed to do, but he also thought he was in charge, and that was where they clashed. Often.

The other two men had the opposite reaction. Johann Hafer and Alan Radanovic were two of the best electronic thieves working today, but even their skills had been no match for the security protocols at Jordan Corp.

Saunders said, "We're talking about the next steps."

Darien nodded.

"After the cockup over Ames," Johann Hafer said, "I say a more direct attack is needed."

Hafer, from northern Germany, wore his straight blond hair in a Beatle cut. The look, popular before he was born, made Darien laugh.

"We tried to hack their systems," Darien said, "and that failed. My strategy is still valid, but we need to find another pigeon."

"Do you have one?" Saunders said.

"Elias Campbell is Jordan's second in

command," she said, "and he has a gambling problem."

"Does he play here?" Saunders asked.

"No. Poker room downtown."

"Well, we also have another situation Alan mentioned before you got here."

Darien looked across the table at Alan Radanovic. He was the quiet one. Didn't speak unless he had something to say, and she found his aloofness irritating. He was skinny, with a sharp jaw and a knob for a chin. Good with a computer, and also a gun.

"What's the problem?" she said.

"Jordan hired help," Saunders said. "He's a guest at the Paramount Hotel on Pine Street, and apparently, he's former CIA."

"How wonderful," Darien exclaimed.

"He needs to be removed."

"Alan can handle that."

"What about Campbell?"

"I will take care of Campbell."

Hafer asked, "And me?"

She smiled at him. "You can babysit your computers, love. I really don't care."

"We start first thing tomorrow," Saunders said. "It's taken too long already."

. . .

SAUNDERS WATCHED DARIEN, Alan, and Johann leave the conference room. The elevator doors rumbled closed, and he was alone.

He started to pace. This wasn't going the way he and the Russian who had brought them all together, Emil Karga, had hoped, which meant his promised bonus was also in jeopardy.

Royal Saunders had been a casino operator for mob interests in Vegas and Atlantic City before the syndicate saw more opportunity and less obvious federal eyes with West Coast Indian casinos. Saunders was shipped west to take care of the mob's work in Seattle.

He wasn't sure of all the details, but when Emil Karga needed a connection in Seattle to handle his hijack crew, Saunders' bosses on the East Coast had handed him the assignment. In return, Karga had promised a significant bonus, but their complications to date and the man hired by Kim Jordan to investigate the problem threatened the whole shebang.

While helping Karga accomplish his mission would help his standing in the Outfit, he hoped its potential failure wouldn't reflect badly on him.

He'd always been a glass-half-empty type, and this case was no different.

LUNCH TURNED into a tour of Seattle's sights of interest then dinner with three glasses of wine for Kim and a couple of Maker's and Cokes for Stiletto. She called her office's car service to come and get them. While they waited outside the restaurant, the talking, laughing, and flirting continued.

They'd talked about growing up and spilled a few secrets, and the prim-and-proper business relationship which had begun the moment Stiletto stepped into her office transformed into something much more casual.

And when Kim returned from the ladies' room before dessert with the top button of her blouse undone, Stiletto couldn't help but notice.

The wind kicked up a little. Kim stepped closer to Stiletto and he put an arm around her.

"We aren't quite dressed for this weather," she said, shaking from the chill. "My legs are freezing."

"I don't know how you stand weather like this."

"It has its moments."

The office car pulled up a few feet away, and

they climbed inside. The driver already had the heater running, and the toasty interior made Kim instantly relax in her seat.

Presently the driver pulled up to her house.

"Feel like a nightcap, Scott?"

"Sure."

To the driver, she said, "Be back in one hour."

"Yes, ma'am."

Kim fumbled with the keys, dropping them, laughing, and moving aside as Stiletto picked them up. She told him which keys to use, and he opened the door.

She snapped on the kitchen light and kicked her shoes off and to the side.

"All I have is wine."

"That's fine," Stiletto said, trying to pierce the darkness of the other rooms. The place was far too clean, but at least the kitchen had a lived-in patina.

She struggled with opening the bottle.

"How much did I drink tonight?" she asked.

Stiletto moved behind her and started massaging her neck.

"Relax for a minute."

"Oh, wow, you have magic fingers," she purred.

Stiletto felt the tension leaving her shoulders and dug in a little more.

"I'm melting."

"You work too hard."

"Mmmm."

"What do you do for fun?"

"Date my showerhead." She let out an embarrassed laugh.

Stiletto stopped and turned her to face him. His arms circled her thin waist, and she didn't argue.

"How long till the car comes back?"

"An hour."

He pulled her closer. "We better not waste it."

They didn't.

THE PHONE RANG.

Stiletto picked up the extension on the nightstand, but only heard a dial tone. He groggily hung up and grabbed his cell.

"What?"

"You're gonna want to see what I found."

Suzi.

"Seriously, turn on your laptop."

"Do you know what time it is?"

"Do you want to earn your pay?"

Stiletto grumbled and turned on the nightstand

light, threw the covers off his naked body, and put down the phone long enough to pull on a bathrobe. Cell phone in hand, he went to the table and booted the laptop.

"Give me a rundown," he told Suzi.

"Were you out all night?"

"Yes. Working hard on the case."

"I bet. Anyway, we got Russians. Well, one."

"Usually all it takes. Laptop is on, now what?"

"Go to your email. I sent a few pictures."

Stiletto made a series of clicks. "Okay. Inside a casino. So?"

Suzi said: "You asked for bad actors, and I found some with a basic sweep of the city to see if anything shook out. Basically, I got lucky. The Golden Willow Casino is O&Oed by Royal Saunders, late of a Las Vegas mob concern. They sent him out here to run the shop."

"Okay."

"Picture number one."

Stiletto clicked the attachment.

"You hacked the security cameras?"

"Easy as pie," Suzi breezed.

"I see a man standing in his office. Saunders?"

"Correct. Picture two."

"Now there's another man."

"Pic three is a zoom."

Stiletto clicked. He whistled.

"When you said one Russian—"

"Yup. Friend of yours, right?"

"Not really. More like a sworn enemy."

The Russian in the picture was Emil Karga, a former Russian agent who'd gone into business for himself, mostly selling guns and sex-trafficking through the Balkans. Back in his CIA days, Stiletto had led a commando strike against Karga's base of operations, only to lose a man and see Karga escape.

"Next pic," Suzi said.

The fourth picture showed a dark-haired woman using the rear entrance. She was perfectly framed in the doorway.

"I'd bet a lobster dinner," Suzi said, "that you're looking at the mysterious lady who doped Harry Ames."

"We'll know for sure when I show him."

"The next several shots are of her going to an elevator, nothing exciting."

"Some good angles, though. What else?"

"Not much. You can see her leaving, but it doesn't look like anybody else is with her."

"It can't be only her and Karga."

"I'll keep checking."

"This was worth waking up for, Suzi. Thanks."

"It's why you pay me."

Stiletto went back to bed but lay awake for a while. Suzi was indeed a great asset. It was almost like the old days.

Almost.

HARRY AMES LOOKED up from some paperwork as Stiletto tapped on his open office door.

"Do you have a moment?"

"Sure," Ames said.

Stiletto showed Ames the pictures on the cell phone.

"Is this the woman you met at the bar?"

Ames took the phone and scrolled through the pictures a couple of times. He examined each photo carefully.

"That's her," he said, handing back the phone. "I can't believe you found her."

"Friends in low places," Stiletto explained.

He left Ames and rode an elevator to Kim Jordan's office. A smile tugged at the corners of his mouth.

She waited for him behind her desk. She was smiling too.

"Good morning."

"Hello," he returned. "Sleep okay?"

She rose from her chair and gave him a soft embrace.

"I had a wonderful night. You know I don't usually—"

"Let's say it was a wonderful night for both of us."

He moved to a chair, and they sat. He explained Suzi's update and showed her the photos on his cell.

"Interesting," she said. "There hasn't been a serious Mafia presence in Seattle since the '70s. There was a big battle between the syndicate and a one-man army who came blazing through to wipe them out, and he pretty much succeeded."

"I think I read about that once," Stiletto said. "But history or not, Saunders is here, and is apparently the local connection for the hijack team."

"It's not the Russians or Chinese?"

"Not the governments, per se. Karga is working on his own. He's a freelancer who will sell to the highest bidder whether it's Russia, China, India, al-

Qaeda, or whoever else places a bid. I know him well."

"You do?"

"He killed a colleague of mine a few years ago."

She blinked. "I'm so sorry."

"I'll settle with him later, don't worry."

"What about right now?"

"I asked you for a list."

"Right." She pulled a yellow legal pad from a drawer. "I thought it best not to have this on my computer."

She said she was mostly concerned with her upper managers, people like Harry Ames, who had the unrestricted access the hijack crew would need. The individual technicians only focused on parts of the radar project, not the whole thing, so trying to use them would be a dead-end. They only had access to their portion of the responsibilities.

Stiletto saw Elias Campbell's name on the list.

"We need to get the woman's picture to everybody and tell them to be on the lookout."

"Okay."

"Where's Campbell now? He's the most likely target since he's your number two."

She picked up her phone and tried to reach

Campbell, with no luck. She spoke briefly with the front desk and put the phone down.

"I'll find him," she said. "He showed up at 8:30, but isn't here now."

"Early lunch?"

"Probably."

Stiletto stood. "I'll be back in a while."

"Where are you going?"

"Gonna try my luck at the slots."

He winked at her.

CHAPTER 7

Suzi called while he was on the road, driving a Jordan Corp. black sedan.

"What do you have now?" he asked.

"Research on Karga," Suzi said. "Lately he's been working with a team. Darien Foster, Johann Hafer, and Adam Radanovic. The latter two are computer experts, and Radanovic has also been involved with contract killing."

"That's our Darien. Thanks, Suzi."

"I'm digging some more. Always on the job!"

Stiletto let out a short laugh.

Darien Foster didn't need to look too hard to find Elias Campbell.

He kept to a regular lunch routine, but she didn't find him at his preferred restaurant.

Her next stop was the Fortune Poker Room.

She had no intention of letting Emil Karga have the anti-stealth radar plans. She had her own agenda. She hated the Russians, all of them, and a chance to strike at Karga's plan to make a hero of himself was too much to resist.

Her joining his gang had required a name change, but that didn't matter. She'd had many names over the years.

There were plenty of governments and individual players who would pay through the nose to get their hands on the radar plans. It was the literal retirement score, and she meant to get her hands on as much of that cash as possible.

She entered the poker room. Even at the noon hour, the tables had heavy play, the room full of clicking chips and the ruffle of cards.

To the left was a small bar where three men sat drinking. Two were having a quiet conversation. The third man sat alone.

Elias Campbell.

He nursed a whiskey and soda and stared into the glass. He wasn't exactly the picture of happiness. Darien smiled to herself. He was at his lowest point. Perfect target.

She confidently made her approach. She'd made sure to wear an eye-catching outfit. He'd look more than once.

She took the stool next to him, practically rubbing a breast on his left elbow, and told the bartender she wanted a double vodka.

Campbell didn't look at her.

Well, that was mildly amusing, she decided.

She asked, "Can't get a game?"

"What?" he said. He turned, and his eyes lingered.

"The club won't let you play, right? Not even a quickie lunchtime game?"

"Who are you?"

The bartender brought the vodka. She took a long drink.

"You owe too much, don't you?"

"I know who you are." Campbell moved his glass away from her. "You drugged a friend of mine."

"He's not really your friend. Right *now* he is since you work together, but when one of you changes jobs, you'll never speak again."

He faced forward. "Go away."

"But I'm here to help. Or, rather, I'll pay you to help me."

"Steal my company's secrets?"

"In return for paying off your debt and more."

"Please leave."

"Elias, if you wanted me to leave so badly, you'd have raised your voice."

"I don't want to make a scene."

"Right, you're in too much trouble here already. How much?"

"Forget it."

"Try two hundred thousand. I know all about your problems, Elias. Wouldn't you like to wipe that out?"

"I'll run it up again."

"You'll be smarter next time. You and I both know that."

"I'm not stealing anything for you."

"Why be loyal to a company that would toss you on the street as soon as it suited them? You're nothing to Jordan, and you know it."

"I'm not going to prison."

"Nobody wants that," Darien said. "You'd only roll over on me, so I don't want that at all."

Darien sipped her vodka and studied Campbell's neck. If he didn't go for this, she'd have to do it the hard way and leave his body somewhere.

He took a drink, and some of the whiskey slopped out one corner of his mouth. He wiped it with a cocktail napkin.

"You need money," Darien said. "I need those stealth radar plans. Surely we can come to an agreement."

She put her right hand on his leg and he stiffened. She moved the hand toward his crotch.

"Seriously, let's work this out. It will benefit both of us."

She started rubbing between his legs.

"I need a million." He shifted on the barstool.

"There you go. Why?" She teased some more with her manicured nails.

"I'll need to disappear."

"I can help with that. I disappear once or twice a month."

Campbell swallowed what remained of his drink and turned to her. "And we do it today. I want the money as soon as we're done."

"You'll have it, and something else to help you relax."

She took her hand away and finished the vodka, then leaned close to his ear.

"I'll be waiting in the ladies' room."

Stiletto wanted to draw the enemy out of its shell.

If they came after him, they'd make the job much easier.

He wandered the busy casino playing random slot machines, armed with the Colt and itching for a chance to use it. He could end Kim's problems before dinner.

Between feeding coins into the one-armed bandits, Stiletto paused to stand in plain view of security cameras and let his face be known. He was counting on being recognized, and that the crew already knew of his comings and goings at Jordan Corp. Once they realized he'd found their hiding place, they'd make a move to grab him.

And then the fun would really begin.

It didn't take long.

Maybe a hair more than an hour.

The man who suddenly stuck to Stiletto like a sweat-soaked shirt had a killer's eyes, vivid but lifeless. They were fixed on Scott, unblinking, like a video camera. He was thin, with sunken cheeks and a knobby, prominent chin.

Radanovic. Had to be. The tweed sports coat, unbuttoned, more than likely concealed his artillery.

Stiletto played another row of slots, plugging his gaming card into each machine as he went along.

Scott visited the restroom, and as he exited, spotted Radanovic nearby. Scott turned right. The hallway led to the casino's restaurant—maybe a thirty-yard walk. The walls were black, as was the carpet, track lighting illuminating the way. Stiletto stopped midway and stepped into an alcove where a door marked SERVICE—NO ADMITTANCE prevented him from going farther, but the alcove effectively hid him from view. He slipped the Combat Government from his shoulder rig.

Radanovic wasn't walking very fast when he passed, using a cluster of oblivious tourists for cover. Scott fell in behind the killer, who turned too late. Stiletto jammed the .45 hard into his back.

"For a professional killer, you really aren't that good," Scott said in the skinny man's ear.

Radanovic replied with a grunt.

"Maybe you aren't professional but convinced everybody you are?"

Stiletto shifted to reach under Radanovic's

right arm, relieved the man of a suppressor-fitted Browning Hi-Power, and stuffed the gun in his waistband.

"Take me to your leader. And remember there's a .45 in your back that can open you up for the whole world to see."

Radanovic said nothing, his jaw clenched tight in defiance, but he turned and, with Stiletto behind him, started walking back to the game room.

WHEN THE ELEVATOR doors slid closed and the cabin started upward, the killer made his move.

Stiletto had expected the attempt, Radanovic backing up to try to pin Scott against the wall, pivoting with his right elbow up for a strike. He moved quickly, his breathing unchanged. Stiletto shoved Radanovic off-balance with his free left hand and brought the cold steel of the Colt down on the man's head in two skin-splitting blows.

Blood splashed on Scott from the open head wound, and Radanovic dropped like a sack of apples. Stiletto stepped back, took out the silenced Browning, and shot the skinny man once in the head. More crimson spatter on his shoes.

Killing was a messy business.

The elevator, halfway up, quickly approached the top floor. Stiletto placed a hurried call to Suzi, telling her to hack the casino cameras again and this time erase the security footage. She didn't ask why.

The cabin stopped and the doors opened on a plush waiting room, beyond which was a pair of double doors.

Scott dragged Radanovic's body partially out of the elevator to keep the doors from closing. To the left was the stairwell. He crossed the waiting area and shot the double-doors open with a trio of slugs from the Hi-Power, then stepped through into a large office.

Royal Saunders, seated at his desk with his back to the wall, rose incredulously.

"Keep those hands on the desk," Stiletto said, putting away the Colt to use the silenced Browning. He centered the muzzle on Saunders' chest.

"My people will be right up," Saunders informed him.

"I hope they'll do better than the chap with the funny chin."

A door crashed open in the waiting room. The stairs. Stiletto spun around. A man breathing hard and clutching a gun ran toward him, most likely

Hafer. He wasn't a very smart man, because he could have shot Stiletto from the doorway. The Browning spat twice, and Hafer looked startled as his white shirt turned red in two places. He hit the carpet in a heap.

That only left the woman, Darien. Where was she?

Stiletto turned back to Saunders, who had a pistol halfway out of a drawer. Another thump from the Hi-Power. The shot split Saunders' right shoulder open and he screamed as he fell, the gun slipping from his grasp and falling to the carpet. His legs struck the chair and knocked it over.

Stiletto kicked away the gun and stood over Saunders, who lay on his wounded side, and shoved him onto his back with a blood-specked shoe. The snout of the Browning was aimed at on Saunders' left eye.

"Where's Karga?" Stiletto asked.

Saunders breathed hard and fast, his face and neck flushed red.

"He's not here."

"You don't deny you know him. Good, you may live yet. Where is he?"

"I'm not—"

Stiletto clamped a foot on the wounded

shoulder and Saunders screamed again. Stiletto lifted his foot and Saunders whimpered a little, curling up on his good side. He wiped his face. When he stopped making noise, Stiletto forced him onto his back again.

"One more time."

Saunders answered between gasps.

"My place. He's at my place. Cabin outside of town."

"Address."

Saunders rattled off the street and number. He might have been lying, but it was easy to check, and once Karga learned his crew had been wiped out, he'd come after Scott hard. Stiletto could sit and wait if he wanted.

But sitting around wasn't something he was very good at.

"Now what?" Saunders asked.

"You're a mob man, Royal. You know what 'no comebacks' means."

Saunders opened his mouth again, but Stiletto shot him in the left eye and forever cut off the mob man's retort.

. . .

STILETTO CALLED Kim Jordan from behind the wheel of the company car.

"Any luck with Campbell?"

"His phone keeps going to voicemail."

"I'll be there ASAP."

Stiletto ended the call. He'd used the bathroom adjoining Saunders' office to wipe the blood off his shoes, but there was nothing he could do about his jacket. Luckily the blood blended with the dark fabric.

Suzi called to say she'd wiped the security footage and told Scott he was a very naughty boy.

"I'm only getting started," he told her. "Check an address for me."

He rattled off the location Saunders had provided.

"See if you can get some satellite pics."

"Okay."

Stiletto pulled into the garage beneath the Jordan Corp. building and made his way to Kim's office, where he found her pacing and biting her nails. She froze when she saw him.

"Are you hurt?"

"It's not my blood." He told her what had happened. "The cops will be all over the Golden

Willow soon, but they will blame this on the mob once they start digging."

"If you're sure."

"The only one left is the woman."

"I keep—"

Her desk phone rang. She snatched up the receiver. "Yes?"

She listened for a moment, and her hand started to shake.

"Okay."

She put the phone down.

To Scott, she said, "Elias entered through the east entrance with a woman. They're in the server room."

"Lock it down," Stiletto said, "and hide this." He handed her the Browning with no explanation and ran out of the office.

CHAPTER 8

Elias Campbell couldn't believe how calm he was as he led Darien Foster into the server room. He should have been a nervous wreck since he was not only throwing away his career but committing espionage, but the only thing he could think about was paying off his debt and getting back to the poker tables. That was all that mattered. With the amount of money Foster was going to pay him, he could do that and much more.

A low buzz filled the small space. Metal racks with server units stacked one atop the other with their forever-blinking rows of green and red lights greeted them.

"Which one?" Darien asked.

"Far corner, over there."

Campbell led her past the racks in the center of the room to one that had a wire mesh cover. From a nearby toolbox, he selected a Philips-head screwdriver and hurriedly removed the four screws holding the cover in place. He set it aside.

Darien reached down her shirt, pulled a small thumb drive from her bra cup, and handed it to Campbell. He plugged the drive into a port and opened a drawer that revealed a keyboard. A small monitor slightly above his head showed a blinking prompt awaiting his typed commands.

Campbell's hands flashed across the keyboard, and soon the server started moving data to the thumb drive, as indicated by a line across the monitor and a percentage count.

Alarms blared, and the lock on the server room door clicked with authority.

"They know!"

Darien opened her purse and lifted out a Glock-18 machine pistol. Campbell's face blanched.

"I'm ready," she told him.

"You didn't say—"

The Glock spat a burst of flame and the salvo cut into Campbell's chest, opening him like an unzipped suitcase. He collapsed, his guts spilling onto the white-tiled floor and the pool of blood beneath him growing.

Darien watched the monitor as the percentage of the download crossed sixty.

The alarm continued to assault her eardrums, but she ignored the noise. She also ignored the door. Anybody coming through would fall to the Glock-18 and its nine-millimeter hollow-points.

Seventy-five percent.

She glanced at Campbell's body. Pathetic fool.

Eighty percent.

The door lock slammed back, and Darien turned and raised her weapon. She held her fire until the door opened and the first uniformed security guard stepped through. A second security man was behind him.

She shot the second man first, tearing off part of his face and head, and used the last rounds in the magazine to kill the first man. They hit the floor with finality.

One hundred percent.

Darien slapped a fresh mag into the machine pistol, grabbed the thumb drive, and returned it to her bra. Stepping over the bodies, she exited the server room.

A hurried run down the hall, and the elevator

started to open. She triggered a burst at the man coming out and crashed through the stairwell door.

Scott Stiletto saw the gun before he set eyes on the woman's face.

He moved back and hit the floor as the burst of slugs tore into the elevator car. He hauled out the Colt as she went down the stairs.

In normal circumstances, Scott would never go smashing through a door to chase somebody. That somebody might be waiting on the other side to shoot him. But he ignored that instinct as he rushed toward the door. Darien Foster needed to get out of the building, and she would not wait. He had to stop her. He didn't want to fail Kim. There might not be a second chance this time.

The stairwell door swung open, and he went through it bent at the waist. No gunfire came his way, but from below, the echo of Darien's pounding feet bounced off the walls. His footfalls, louder, joined the cacophony of noise in the narrow stairwell.

The alarm cut off as he started down with his grip tight on the .45, he noticed. A burst of nine-millimeter hornets split the air near him and bounced off handrails, breaking into lead bits that flew everywhere and nicked his clothes.

He'd need a new suit by the time this mission was over.

Stiletto continued his descent at a fast pace, sometimes skipping a few steps by leaping onto a landing. By the third time, the shock to his feet and knees was too much, and he wasn't any closer to her.

Ten floors to go.

He leaned over the railing once to look at the chasm below, the bottom of the shaft. Darien appeared as she rounded another flight and Stiletto fired once, the boom of the shot deafening. The round struck behind her heel on the steel step with only an ineffectual spark.

Stiletto continued down, breathing hard. If he missed a step or slipped, he'd go face-first onto a concrete landing, which would put him out of action.

Another flight down. Six floors left. How was security situated in the lobby? How was she planning to make her getaway?

Four floors. Stiletto's lungs burned, and his heart felt like it was going to explode out of his chest. He mentally pushed the discomfort away.

One more flight. Darien reached the lobby door, and he fired again and hit the doorframe. Darien yelped but didn't stop, and then the machine pistol sounded like a buzz-saw as she opened fire.

THREE SECURITY GUARDS waited for her in the lobby with about six feet between them. They were armed with Remington 870 pump shotguns, but they looked too green to use them effectively. They were used to a cushy job, not experienced in combat.

Darien grinned at the hesitation in their eyes as she aimed the Glock.

She ran toward the guards who stood between her and the glass front of the building. Her first burst took down the middle man as he shouldered his shotgun. The weapon fired a wasted charge into the floor.

She swung her aim left and the next burst punched through guard number two's chest, splitting his uniform tie in half and blowing open his upper body. Some of the rounds over-penetrated and shattered the glass window behind him.

Another gun went off behind her and she

gasped as her left elbow burned, the shot splitting open skin but continuing on. She whirled and dropped to a knee, triggering rounds as her pursuer left the stairwell door. He dove and slid across the floor.

The man chasing her knew his business.

She turned and fired at the last guard as his shotgun boomed. The hot pellet blast passed too close for comfort, but her rounds scored, knocking the man flat.

Another shot from behind nicked the right cuff of her jeans as Darien ran for the shattered window and leaped through the opening. Her shoes hit the pavement, and she sprinted through the plaza for the parking lot.

STILETTO HAD no time to check the fallen guards, and there was probably nothing he could do for them anyway.

He ran across the lobby, heading for the same opening she had used, but as he tried to move around the fallen guard in front of it, his shoes slipped in the man's blood. He fell forward, tumbled painfully through the opening, and rolled onto the pavement and into the bushes on the other side. He couldn't ignore the pain this time and let out a yell. As he unevenly gained his feet, a car screeched out of the adjacent parking lot used by low-level staff and visitors and swung into the flow of traffic.

Scott, out of gas, lay on his stomach and willed away the pain screaming through every part of his body.

For well into the night, Jordan Corp. crawled with cops and crime-scene crews, as well as federal representatives who made their presence unavoidable.

Stiletto lay on the leather couch in Kim Jordan's office, where an FBI agent took him through his story several times. Kim had ordered him to hold nothing back. Another agent spoke to her as she paced near her desk, a bundle of nervous energy.

Finally, when they were alone, he rose from the couch and went over to her. He winced as she fell into his arms and she gasped, apologizing, as she put him back on the couch, sitting at the far end to cradle his head in her lap. She had a soft lap.

"I'm sorry," he said.

"You tried." She stroked his hair.

"The feds will have to step in now."

"I know."

"Will you be okay?"

"I don't know. Poor Elias—"

The tears finally broke through her tough exterior. Stiletto sat up, scooted close, and pulled her to him.

"Everything my father worked for—"

"Hey, it's not over yet."

"They're going to shut me down."

"Not if we get the data back."

"How—"

"Leave that to me. My people are already working on it.

She wiped her eyes. "Your people?"

"Well, person. But Suzi is really good. She'll know Darien's life story by morning, and I'll pick up her trail."

"Scott, you can't. It's too dangerous. Let the government do it."

"They take forever, and that will be too late."

She stopped crying and said nothing for a moment.

"I'll get the data back before they can sell it and put it back in your hands. I swear."

"Promise you won't get hurt."

"Of course." He nudged her away. "I gotta get back to the hotel and clean up."

"Will you stay with me tonight? We can get your things first. I don't want to be alone." She nuzzled his heck. "My bed's big enough for two."

"I know." He gave her a squeeze. "Okay. Come on, let's go."

WHILE STILETTO SHOWERED AWAY the aches and pains, Kim Jordan called her department heads and told them to tell their people not to go to work the next day but remain available if the cops or feds wanted to talk.

By the time Stiletto crawled into bed next to her warm body, she was fast asleep.

He lay awake listening to her breathe, running the next steps in the chain through his mind.

He'd call Suzi in the morning and talk about any possible leads, then he'd need to arrange transportation out of the country to wherever that next lead appeared.

He wouldn't rest until he got the data back and returned it to Kim.

Another victory he needed, like the el-Gad hit all over again.

Would that need ever go away?

After a while, he drifted off to sleep.

STILETTO STOOD on the porch the next morning as he spoke to Suzi, smoking a Montecristo. Kim didn't mind. She said the scent of the cigar smoke reminded her of Dad.

"Tell me you got something," he said.

"Oh, I got, all right," Suzi replied. "But do you know what time it is here?"

"Do you want to get paid?"

"Touché. Listen up. Darien Foster isn't her real name. She was born Zhanna Petrova in Moscow in 1979. Her parents were high-ranking KGB officers who were murdered when she was ten."

"Why?"

"Accused traitors," Suzi explained. "After that, she lived with relatives and got into gangs, and eventually the Russian Mafia. Her first reported kill was the man who had ordered her parents' deaths."

"And?"

"Wanted by the FSB, and *persona non-grata* in

Russia. She hooked up with a man named Franko St. Regis, and together they run a small crime syndicate with fingers in a lot of pies—human trafficking, narcotics, and contract murder."

"Where's St. Regis now?"

"No idea, but I have inquiries out."

"I need to get those plans back. Jordan still has the primary files, but that won't matter if somebody else buys the plans."

"I have one lead that might work."

"I'm listening," Stiletto said.

"Primo Fortunado. Italian smuggler. Ring any bells?"

Stiletto thought for a moment. The name sounded familiar, but he didn't recall specific details. One thing he did remember, though.

"Daughter named Nikki, right?"

"Correct. They have a contract out on Foster and St. Regis for hijacking one of their gun shipments. She shot Primo in the knee, and he's been crippled ever since. They're involved with drugs and illegal gambling too. Perfect angels, right? Anyway, he might be willing to suggest a course of action."

"Where are they?"

"Sicily."

"Then that's where I'm going next."

"I'll email more details."

Stiletto hung up. Kim opened the door and told him she had bacon and eggs ready, and Scott left his cigar on the porch and followed her inside. He was starving.

AFTER BREAKFAST and reading Suzi's email, Stiletto made two more calls to arrange transportation to Catania, Sicily. Suzi's information said the Fortunados lived on the coast near the airport because Primo liked to watch the jets take off and land.

Kim drove Scott back to his hotel. She pulled up on the street but made no move to get out. Her hands remained tight on the wheel.

"This is it?" she asked, turning to him.

"For now," Scott told her. A quick kiss and he left the car, leaning back to say: "See you soon."

He shut the door and didn't look back as he entered the hotel. If he had looked back, his resolve might have weakened. It would be easy to stay and let somebody else do the dirty work. Why did it have to be him? But he'd made a promise, and he intended to keep it.

He could spend the rest of the day dwelling on Kim, but he forced her from his mind. If he accomplished the mission, then maybe he'd think about her some more, but the idea brought to mind Ali Lewis in San Francisco.

He hadn't gone back to her despite her job offer and a chance at something more. Why did he think he'd remain with Kim Jordan longer than Ali Lewis?

He wondered if the Fortunados would even bother to help. If they had actionable information on Darien Foster, they'd act on it and save the contract money. Then again, maybe they wouldn't, in order to spare their own resources.

He'd have to find a way to persuade them if he met any hesitation.

Stiletto rode an elevator to his floor and walked down the hall. Something smelled funny—a waft of sharp cologne. He'd smelled the cologne once before, and instinct made him take out the Colt .45 as he slipped the key card into the electronic lock of his hotel room door.

The door opened, and there was nothing else to do but toss the .45 on the carpet. The gun landed with a hard thump.

"Good choice, Mr. Stiletto."

One man sat at the table, legs crossed, absently shuffling a deck of cards.

Another man stood near the door to the bathroom holding a SIG-Sauer P-226 automatic on Stiletto's midsection.

The man at the table, with a pointed goatee, prominent cheekbones, and dark eyes, put down the cards.

"Did you forget about me?" Emil Karga asked. "I didn't forget about you."

Stiletto stared at the man, the Russian renegade who had initiated the Jordan Corp. theft, ignoring the other man, who held a gun.

"You've been busy. I'm sure I slipped your mind." He offered Scott a cruel smile that quickly faded. Karga said, "Shut the door. We don't want to disturb the other guests."

CHAPTER 9

Scott Stiletto kicked the door closed.

"Put up your hands. Not all the way, just to your shoulders. No tricks."

Stiletto complied. Karga started shuffling the cards again and laid out a round of solitaire.

"Most people play that on their phones now," Stiletto said.

"We aren't most people," Karga replied.

"What do you want?"

"Where is she?"

"Who?"

"Darien Foster. She has something I was supposed to take delivery of. Notice I'm not vain enough to say it belongs to me."

"You're vain enough to point that out," Stiletto told him.

Karga chuckled as he put a card down, setting another aside.

"It will be a shame to kill you. You're the only one who calls out my nonsense."

"I don't know where she went, but I'm going to find out."

Karga looked at Stiletto with a mischievous spark behind his eyes. "No, you're not."

Stiletto took a deep breath. His nerves remained steady. He might not have had his pistol, but Karga's number two was standing way too close.

"It's so hard to find good help these days," Karga said, going back to his game. He lined up another card and discarded two. "Darien and her friends were supposed to be very good at their jobs. Meet my assistant, Mr. Killkin."

Stiletto laughed.

The gunman said, "My name is not funny."

Killkin filled his suit the way a linebacker might, and his hair was shaggy. His neck vanished beneath the shirt collar.

"The hell it isn't," Stiletto said. "Talk about being typecast, you poor bastard."

Killkin's grip tightened on the pistol.

"Count to ten, Killkin," Karga suggested.

Stiletto said, "So, are we teaming up or something?"

"You want to kill me."

"Sure."

"Somehow a truce doesn't fit your personality."

"Correct. I'd shoot you in the back at some point. But we have to move this along a little. My arms are getting tired."

"We'll kill you in the bathtub and take our leave."

"Your boyfriend doesn't have a silencer on that gun."

Karga raised his head from the cards and regarded the wall thoughtfully, then gathered the cards and returned them to a box taken from a jacket pocket. "That *is* a problem," he said. "Killkin, render Mr. Stiletto unconscious, and you may kick him twice after."

The killer raised his gun and stepped closer. Stiletto planted his right foot and launched a kick with his left aimed for Killkin's stomach. The textbook blow landed where Stiletto wanted, but he winced as pain flashed through his leg. He might as well have kicked a brick wall. Killkin at least showed some discomfort via a twisted expression, but then he swung the automatic. Stiletto fell like a dropped piano and remained conscious long enough to feel the first of Killkin's two kicks.

But only the first.

STILETTO WOKE UP SWEATY, his body jammed in a small compartment. He was locked in a trunk.

His body didn't hurt for about thirty seconds, and then the blow to the head, the two kicks to the ribs, and the residual aches from the night before began competing to see who could make him hurt the most.

Thankfully the car traveled along a smooth surface, at least for now. Karga and Killkin were probably taking him to the woods outside the city. It would have been a shame to ruin a perfectly good hotel room anyway.

He started moving his hands. They were bound behind his back with a plastic zip-tie that dug into his skin, but the tie wasn't as tight as it might have been. They'd applied the restraint in a hurry, possibly after they'd stuffed him in the trunk. He wondered idly how they'd removed him from the hotel and decided it had probably been through the back exit, Karga and Killkin supporting him between them as if he were drunk. They'd have stopped later in a safe spot to move him to the trunk and tie his wrists, which explained why his hands weren't numb.

He wanted to chuckle, but his body hurt too much. Instead, he rolled onto his left arm, hard to do since his legs, bent at the knees, were bumping the side of the trunk. He started painfully working his fingers into the inside of his belt, where a slit compartment contained a razor blade hidden for emergencies exactly like this one.

He winced, biting his lip to stifle a groan, his fingers opening the compartment and touching the warm steel. Slowly, he pulled it free and rotated it so the sharp edge rested against the plastic strip.

The car jolted as it went over a pothole, his body bounced with the impact, and the razor slipped from his grasp. Stiletto rolled onto his back, breathing hard. Terrific.

Then the car slowed and made a turn. The speed remained low, maybe thirty miles per hour, but the bumps were constant, rocking him back and forth. Stiletto couldn't hold back the grunts. Hopefully they couldn't hear. He needed them to believe he was still out cold. Some invisible being was using his head for a bongo drum. He only wanted to stay as motionless as possible. They'd kill him if he didn't find an edge. He rolled onto his left side again and felt for the razor, but his fingers brushed only the trunk's thin carpet. His pulse quickened. *Slow down. Don't panic. Feel carefully.*

He shifted a little and tried again, and finally, he found the blade, forcing his body to move in the confined space so he could get the proper grip. *There. Got it.* Stiletto started to move the blade in a slow sawing motion, then a bump forced the sharp edge into his right palm and he bit back a scream. *Stop. Now try again.* He resumed sawing as he felt blood roll down his fingertips.

The zip-tie snapped and he brought his hands to his chest, his right hand slick with blood. The bumpy ride continued. *Break's over, look around.* His eyes scanned the dark and felt around for a possible weapon, but the trunk was empty except for him. Totally clean. No clutter whatsoever. And then his eyes froze on the trunk lid. Or, rather, something glowing green near the latch.

Stiletto allowed a short laugh. Car companies had taken to installing emergency release mechanisms in trunks because, apparently, people found themselves locked within them quite frequently.

What had seemed like more government safety nonsense was now a blessing.

He automatically reached with his right hand, but the pain stopped him. He pulled the hand back and held it close to his chest. He'd only have a few seconds once the lid lifted.

He used his left hand to pull the release lever, and the trunk lid popped open. An indicator light would be flashing on the dash now.

Stiletto shoved the lid all the way up and rolled over the back, landing hard on the rough pavement as the car jerked to a stop. Stiletto bolted to the shoulder and into the forest ahead, Karga and Killkin shouting, pops from the SIG pistol splitting the afternoon air. The shots zipped through the foliage as Stiletto's shoes pounded the soft earth.

The shooting stopped. They'd be coming after him, so Stiletto kept running, weaving around trees and fallen trunks. The ground inclined and Stiletto started breathing harder, his body straining with the effort. Then his legs gave out and he fell to the ground. *Gotta...keep moving.* But his body wouldn't respond, and the footsteps of his pursuers grew louder. He rolled left, stopping at a trunk and reaching for a fallen branch that looked solid. His right hand burned as he wrapped his fingers around it and he tried to stop the yell that forced its way out but failed. All sounds ceased.

Stiletto moved the branch to his left hand and looked at his wounded right. It wasn't a bad cut; he could tough out the pain. He put the branch back in his right and clamped his mouth shut as the cut burned. He could shoot with his left, but not swing a bat that way.

He stayed flat and listened. As far as he knew, only Killkin had a gun. Unless he'd changed his habits, Karga wasn't known to carry one.

Twigs snapped and leaves crackled. Stiletto shivered from the afternoon chill, and then he saw Killkin.

The man was ten feet away, holding his gun casually. He knew his quarry was wounded and unarmed. Stiletto stayed flat. He wanted the tree to cover him as long as possible, but the numbers were falling fast, and there'd be no protection from the thick trunk for much longer.

Killkin made a right and headed down the incline. The move made sense. He'd expect Scott to take the path of least resistance. He had all day to retrace his steps if he guessed wrong.

Stiletto's eyes darted around. No sign of Karga.

He was probably still at the car playing solitaire on the hood.

Stiletto willed his body to move, forcing his knees under him, then rising slowly so as not to make any noise. He kept his eyes fixed on Killkin's back, which was now maybe fifteen or twenty feet away. The Russian killer was moving slowly too, scanning for any sign of Scott.

Stiletto broke into a run, ignoring the painful protests from every limb. The decline increased his speed and he brought up the branch over his shoulder, hoping Killkin's neck wasn't as hard as his stomach.

Killkin spun around, firing a wild shot that zinged past Stiletto's left ear as he swung as hard as he could. The blow hit Killkin solidly in the temple. He uttered a short scream and toppled over. Stiletto tripped on his body and fell hard again, the breath knocked out of him, but he scrambled back. Killkin was moving to get up as well. Stiletto landed on him, forcing the Russian onto his back, then pressing the branch into his thick neck and pushing all of his weight down.

Guttural noises came from Killkin's throat and he thrashed and landed ineffectual blows on Scott, but Stiletto kept the pressure on. When the thrashing stopped, Stiletto rolled off the man's body and scooped up his lost automatic. Stiletto fired once, Killkin's head splitting like a watermelon and spraying bits of gore all over the forest floor.

Renewed strength surged through Scott, the elation of being alive fueling him as he headed back toward the road.

Spotting the gold Honda sedan through the trees, Stiletto braced against a tree, still breathing hard but aiming at Karga, who stood near the passenger door anxiously scanning the forest.

Stiletto fired. The shot missed and Karga started to run, and Scott fired again. He reached the road before Karga cleared the opposite shoulder and fired again and again, his left arm shaking. None of the rounds connected and Karga vanished into the trees, footsteps quickly fading.

Stiletto, gasping, dropped to hands and knees beside the car. After a moment, he opened the passenger door. Karga had left his jacket on the passenger seat, and had left the key fob in the center console.

Scott drove away after tossing Karga's deck of cards out the window as hard as he could.

. . .

THE JACKET WAS TOO small to wear, but Scott carried it back into the hotel to hide his hand. He entered through the rear to avoid the lobby and forced himself up the back stairs to his floor.

The key card to get in had remained in his pocket the whole time, the left pocket, thankfully, and Stiletto shut the door. He stumbled into the bathroom without turning on the light and ran water over his right hand, rinsing away blood and grit, then gently using soap to finish the job.

Turning on the light and grabbing a small first-aid kit from under the sink, he applied rubbing alcohol, the sting making him dizzy with pain, and slapped on a bandage.

Then he turned to the toilet and vomited violently. He remained over the toilet for a few moments, getting his breath back, then rinsed his mouth with cold water and trudged to the bed. He fell onto the mattress and passed out.

THE NEXT MORNING, he felt a little better.

A flurry of calls rescheduled his departure, and he showered, pulled on some clean clothes, and quickly packed. He retrieved the Colt from the floor, and secured the pistol in the x-ray-proof bottom of his suitcase.

He changed his bandage and put a few spares in his pocket. The cut wasn't bad and didn't look like it needed stitches.

After a light breakfast in the hotel restaurant, which brought more strength back to him, he took a cab to the airport where his charter waited.

Next stop: Sicily.

STILETTO DOZED off and on throughout the flight, sitting alone in an air-conditioned cabin with soft carpet and plush leather seats, Wi-Fi, satellite tv, and alcohol. He would have enjoyed the amenities had he not felt like a wreck, so the fourteen-hour flight and rest was welcome.

He hated that Karga had escaped again, but with the radar plans in the open, their paths were sure to cross once more.

When the jet touched down, Scott was awake and eager to get back in the fight. He could at least make a fist with his right hand now. Whether or not the checkered walnut grips of the .45 would agitate the cut was the question. He could always adjust his shoulder rig for a left-hand draw.

Customs at Vincenzo Bellini Airport didn't take long, and Stiletto carried his case into the main terminal as he made for the exit, eyeing a line of taxis parked outside.

This was his first visit to Catania, Sicily, although he'd been active on the opposite side of the island many times. Catania was Sicily's second largest city and the spot where Stiletto hoped to get a lead on Darien Foster or whoever she really was. Stiletto wondered how many identities she had at the ready and whether or not another name change would slow his pursuit. Somebody like Primo Fortunado, the Italian smuggler who held a grudge and had a kill contract out on Darien's life, might be able to sort through Darien's chaff.

If Scott could convince him.

Stiletto was barely midway to the exit when he spotted the two men following him. They moved casually, dressed in street clothes with light jackets, but they moved like soldiers. Their eyes stayed focused on Scott. One had a thick head of black hair, the other bushy black eyebrows.

Stiletto shook his head and kept moving. The opposition would not take him out in public. They might, however, try at his hotel.

He gave the cab driver the name of his hotel,

and the driver pulled away from the curb. Traffic in front of the terminal was metered by three stop lights at equal intervals, and when the cab finally cleared the terminal and cruised along the access road to the main streets, Scott glanced back. No cars followed. Whoever those two men were, they had to have been stopped by the last traffic light.

Stiletto had booked a room not far from the beach. He planned to make his approach to the Fortunado house on foot.

The hotel sat on a hill overlooking the beach and crashing waves. The street in front of the hotel, Vale Presidente Kennedy, made Stiletto raise an eyebrow as he paid the driver.

He paused at the steps to look at the ocean again, bright sun reflecting off the water and the air warm with a gentle breeze. It was the exact opposite of Seattle, and he loved it. What he did not love were the structures, homes mostly, that took up a lot of the beach space. Oh, well. Stiletto hustled up the steps with only a little discomfort and found a friendly young woman behind the check-in desk who helped him get squared away. She told him the hotel restaurant didn't open for another two hours.

Stiletto laughed as he unpacked. He'd have to

buy some clothes. His suit had been ruined chasing Darien Foster at Jordan Corp., and a pair of jeans and a blue button-down wrecked in the forest. The job was getting expensive as far as his wardrobe went.

He opened the patio doors to let in the breeze and ocean noise.

Stiletto frowned, thinking of the two men at the airport. Darien's people? Or had Fortunado sent them after hearing about Stiletto's arrival via the underworld grapevine?

After getting the .45 and shoulder rig from his case, he tested a couple of draws with his right hand. It was acceptable as long as the bandage didn't get torn up when he fired. Stiletto loaded three magazines and put the gun back in the case.

CHAPTER 10

STILETTO HANDED the menu back to the waiter; he'd decided on linguine with clam sauce. The hotel restaurant had filled up quickly once he was seated, the conversation level quickly rising.

He scanned faces but saw nobody paying any attention to him. He sat with his back to a wall, which kept him away from the hub of activity and provided the perfect view of the entryway and bar.

The waiter brought his Maker's and Coke and Scott took an appreciative sip. He'd had more close calls in Seattle than he wanted to admit, and it felt really good to be in one piece and sipping good whiskey so close to the ocean.

It was hard not to feel lonely as he watched couples and friends enjoying each other's company. There he was, alone, living out of a suitcase. But he did notice a lone woman at the bar. She stood instead of making use of a stool, held a glass of red wine carefully, and stared right at him. Stiletto grinned and raised his glass. The opposition had sent a real babe this time. Long dark hair cascading down her shoulders and back, curvy in all the right places, full lips painted red, and the smoldering dark eyes all Sicilian women seemed to possess. The woman detached from the bar and carried her glass to Scott's table. She sat without invitation and leaned toward him.

"You don't want to eat here."

"I don't?"

"The chef wouldn't know good linguine if you fed it to him. You want to come with me."

"Better food at your place?"

"No, you just want to come with me."

"I could take that two ways, you know." Stiletto grinned.

"I'm not fooling around, Mr. Stiletto. Neither are my men. Look at the entrance."

The woman kept her eyes on Scott, sipping her wine as Stiletto's eyes shifted to where she'd indicated. The two men from the airport waited there, one waving off the hostess who asked if they wanted a table.

"Darien didn't send you," Stiletto said. "There's no room for two alpha dogs in her outfit."

"Some call me the alpha *bitch*, but you may call me Nikki."

"Fortunado?"

"That's my father's name. I shorten it to Fortune."

"You're earning yours, right?"

"Not as fast as I'd like. Finish your drink. I already canceled your order."

"What's for dinner at your place?"

"That depends on what kind of conversation we have."

"You probably already know the story. Why the act?"

"You'll find out soon enough. Drink up."

Stiletto toasted her and downed the Maker's and Coke. Nikki Fortune rose from her seat, and Stiletto followed as she marched to the exit. There were worse views to be stuck behind. Nikki's backside was a very pleasant one indeed.

THE ONE WITH the bushy eyebrows drove and the

other sat in the passenger seat. Scott and Nikki sat in the back. They were heading for the ocean. Nobody spoke.

They had not taken his gun or asked him to surrender the weapon, and he didn't ask why. He looked ahead and absently rubbed the bandage on his right hand.

"What happened to your hand?" Nikki Fortune said.

He turned to her. She was looking at him. Those hot eyes missed nothing.

"I sliced it with a razor."

"Why?"

"Nothing good on television."

She didn't laugh. "You make a habit of self-mutilation?"

"Gotta practice on somebody."

"You think you're funny, don't you?"

"Admit it, you're laughing on the inside. I won't tell."

Her shell of a face finally cracked a small smile.

"I'm not as frigid as I seem."

"I never said you were."

"You know what it's like to be in command, right?"

"Sure."

"That's all it is."

"You're being rather vulnerable, Nikki."

She faced forward as the driver made a right turn, the ocean on the left now and partially obscured by the structures on the beach.

"I have my moments," she murmured.

"On a whole other subject, who in the world decided to build those houses on the beach?"

"American celebrities."

"That explains everything."

The car slowed and drove up an inclined driveway that quickly leveled off in front of a home Stiletto would not associate with a smuggler of Primo Fortunado's stature. One story, L-shaped, with the two-car garage in the ninety-degree angle. Modest brick walls, and an outside patio with its table and chairs covered by large collapsible umbrellas.

"Why are you frowning?" Nikki asked.

"I expected a bigger place."

"My father has simple tastes."

"You, on the other hand?"

"Oh, my future mansion will be absolutely obscene."

The car stopped, and the driver shut off the motor. The man in the passenger seat exited and walked around the back to open Nikki's door. She winked at Scott as she swung her long legs out and stepped onto the driveway.

Stiletto opened his own door and as he stepped out, the afternoon breeze dried the sweat on his neck. He hadn't realized he'd *been* sweating. He told himself this was a normal meeting, nothing to worry about. They had no reason to suspect him of any duplicity.

The four headed up the steps to the porch, the driver in the lead, the other behind, with Scott and Nikki in between.

Primo Fortunado met them in the entryway. The man was tall, white-headed, and trim, with a bit of muscle showing under a blue silk shirt left untucked from perfectly-creased slacks. He leaned on a cane on his right side.

Nikki went forward and kissed her father on the left cheek. The two silent bodyguards went elsewhere through a doorway, but Stiletto kept his eyes on Primo rather than look to see what the guards were doing.

"Papa, this is Scott Stiletto."

"You're Italian?" Primo asked.

"Father's side. Mother's Irish."

"What part of Italy is your family from?" He

had the same smoldering eyes as his daughter, and they were fixed on Scott like a pair of cannons.

"I'm sorry to say I'm not sure."

"A man should know where he comes from."

"My brother has all that information. He loves the research."

"But you, on the other hand. . ."

"I waste time on cars and cigars."

Primo laughed. "Well, at least we have one thing in common."

One of the bodyguards, the one with the bushy eyebrows, appeared in the doorway and actually spoke. It was a short sentence, and Scott resisted the urge to tell him good job and feed him a treat.

"Refreshments on the front deck," Primo said and told Nikki, "Bring my cigars."

"Yes, Papa."

While Nikki moved away at a brisk pace, Primo and the guard took Stiletto out to the front patio where the guard with the thick black hair waited by the table. Three mixed drinks sat on the glass top. Primo directed Stiletto to one of the chairs, he took another. Nikki returned with a large humidor and sat in the third.

Stiletto looked at his glass, which held Maker's and-Coke. They knew a lot about him.

Primo offered a toast, and they clinked glasses. The elder Fortunado had what looked like a gimlet, while Nikki's glass appeared to contain straight vodka. Scott certainly didn't think it was plain water.

Stiletto knew better than to talk first, so he glanced at the ocean. The umbrellas above kept the glare of the sun from his eyes.

"You like the ocean, Mr. Stiletto?" Primo asked.

"Looking at it, yes. I get seasick when I'm on a boat."

"Have a Havana," Primo said, offering the open humidor.

Scott selected a Cohiba with a light tan wrapper, and after Primo handed him a cutter and lighter, Stiletto snipped the back and lit the foot. After two starting puffs, he handed the items back to Primo, who lit his own and eased back in the chair.

Nikki's nose crinkled as smoke drifted her way. She waved a hand in front of her face.

"My daughter thinks my Havanas are a disgusting habit."

"They are, Papa."

Stiletto said, "The thing about cigars, though, is

that when you light one, it feels like you've conquered a country."

Primo smiled. He had very white teeth. "You understand," he said. "And how many countries have you conquered?"

"Right now, I'm happy to keep the hounds at bay."

Primo scoffed and raised his hands, shaking his head. "Everybody wants my money for something! Sometimes it's like they make more from my work than I do."

Stiletto laughed in agreement and swallowed some of his drink.

"But enough about our money problems," Primo said. "You came to see us about a mutual enemy."

"I'm impressed," Scott said, "by how you picked me up so quickly. I was going to come up and knock on the door."

Primo laughed. He offered no insight on how they'd known of his arrival, and Stiletto didn't press. The compliment was enough to please Primo's ego.

"Any enemy of Zhanna Petrova is a friend of mine," Primo told him.

"I know her under another name," Stiletto said,

and filled in the Fortunados on the Jordan Corp. situation, without too many specifics. He referred to the anti-stealth radar plans only as "military secrets."

"What makes you think we can help?" Primo asked. "Yes, we have a contract out on her, but nobody has collected yet."

"You might not know where she is, but you know more about her than I do. You probably know her organization better than any police department."

"If we know these things, why not take advantage? Why pay somebody to kill her?"

Stiletto blew out a stream of smoke that the wind carried away from Nikki.

"Because diverting men and resources to take care of the problem is too risky for you. Your men might not make it back, and then your business will suffer. Plus, it might draw unwanted attention, and you have enough of that to deal with.

"I, on the other hand, am not thinking like that. If she has a syndicate she shares with Franko St. Regis, I can smash it. Every single piece. After she hurts enough, she'll come after me."

Nikki jumped in. "I have always argued this.

She crippled my father and took a lot of money from us."

"I am no cripple," Primo said. "What I have is the ability to tell when it's about to rain." He laughed.

Nikki glared at him. "That isn't funny, Papa."

Stiletto said, "Tell me what you know. I'll take care of the contract, and you can keep the money."

Primo frowned. "This is personal for you?"

"Very much so."

"Vendettas are dangerous," Primo remarked without irony.

"I have a promise to keep."

Primo took a deep breath and let it out. "A promise, I can understand."

"To a lover?" Nikki asked, eyes on Scott.

"Are you jealous?"

Her face flushed red.

"Zhanna Petrova," Primo began, "has many areas of operation, but the worst one is on an island off the coast of Greece. Private dock, warehouse, lots of men. She brings women from the Balkans and Africa there on ships, then they're put on trucks and taken who knows where for horrible things. It is a large source of income for her. That's where I'd start."

"Do you have any pictures of the place?" Stiletto asked.

Primo nodded. "And a map."

"She ever there?"

"No."

Nikki stated, "I'm going with him, Papa."

"No," Primo repeated.

"This is our fight too, and we can't deny ourselves the chance."

"No."

"Papa, you know I'm going with or without your permission."

"Listen to your father, Nikki."

Her hot eyes bored into Stiletto.

"Who the hell are you? My family honor is at stake, and you need help. What if your mercenary friends refuse?"

"I wasn't going to call them," Stiletto said.

"Well, Papa?"

"It's too dangerous, sweetheart."

Stiletto said, "I don't need you."

"But I have contacts, too," she shot back. "I can get men who will do anything I tell them."

"For how much?"

"You let *me* worry about that. We will use *my* money."

Primo watched his daughter through a haze of cigar smoke and she turned to stare back, a silent battle of wills that Stiletto found fascinating. He would never have spoken to his father the way she had.

He could use the help, he had to admit, but he didn't trust her. She wanted to build her own fortune, she'd told him, and perhaps she had the idea of taking the "military secrets" for her own gain. It would be a shame to have to stop her too. Scott didn't want Primo Fortunado as an enemy.

"Well, Papa?"

It was almost a taunt.

Primo looked at Scott. "She *could* be an asset."

Or just an ass, Stiletto thought. He'd have to keep an eye on her. He didn't need Nikki Fortune trailing him and trying to sabotage his efforts, if that was what she had in mind. There was nothing to stop her from searching for Darien Foster on her own.

"Okay," Stiletto agreed. "But I want to leave in the morning."

"I'll make some calls." Nikki left the table, her vodka barely touched.

Primo waited until she'd gone back into the house. His eyes never left Stiletto's.

"She is so much like her mother."

"I'll watch out for her."

Primo scoffed and waved a hand. "You won't need to. Just watch your own back."

He knows her well. Stiletto tossed back the last of his drink.

"How are you fixed for weapons?" Primo asked.

Stiletto opened his coat and showed Fortunado the .45 in the shoulder rig. "Only this."

"What else would you like?"

"A Colt Model 933 might be nice, or an M-4. Maybe some grenades."

"We can handle that. We can get you anything short of a bazooka." He shrugged. "They've been hard to come by lately."

"How about a few extra Cohibas, too?"

Primo grinned. "I will do that." He pushed the humidor to Scott and told him to help himself.

Somewhere South of Greece

THE YACHT SLICED through the choppy waters of the Aegean Sea, Greece on one side and Turkey on the other. One of the small stray islands nestled between was the destination of the twenty men, and one woman, aboard the yacht.

Stiletto, standing near the bow, protected from seasickness by Dramamine, scanned the darkness ahead through a pair of Sightmark Ghost Hunter night-vision binoculars. The water and distant terrain had a greenish glow in the viewfinders, but there were no other ships to interfere with the yacht.

Nikki had certainly delivered on the gun crew, the men hardened fighters from various hot spots around the world. They were all belowdecks.

Scott had received the Colt M933 he'd asked for. The 933 was a much shorter version of the M-16 rifle, with an eleven-inch barrel and a collapsible stock. The full-power .223 cartridges in the twenty-round magazine provided plenty of punch.

The weapon wasn't his only piece of gear. The heavy pack over his shoulders contained C-4 and thermite bombs. He wanted to level the warehouse and everything inside—after they'd collected suitable intelligence, of course.

Icy wind cut through the parts of his skin not covered by body armor and black combat fatigues, and cold blasts of water pelted his face like pieces of rock.

Nikki Fortune, her hair tied back and wearing a black combat suit much like Stiletto's, came up beside him. He had to admit she wore the outfit well.

"Captain says another five minutes," she told him, raising her voice over the wind. Her ponytail whipped in the wind.

He handed her the binoculars, and she looked at the target.

"Warehouse looks dark," she said.

"I thought the same thing," Stiletto agreed.

She handed back the binoculars.

"Even if there's nobody there, we'll find something."

"Says who?" Scott asked.

"Is the glass half-full or half-empty?"

Stiletto stowed the binoculars on his combat belt.

"I've always figured it didn't matter," he said. "You work with what you have."

Two minutes. The mercenary crew began moving from below to the top deck. Stiletto, still near the bow, examined the warehouse with his naked eyes, but the building remained dark. The surrounding parking lot also looked empty. The jetty leading from the water onto the asphalt appeared as promised on Primo's map and notes— wooden, wet, and potentially slippery. Stiletto wiped condensation from his forehead. He hadn't come all the way around the world to ride in a boat, which he hated anyway, to go home empty-handed.

The captain cut the engine and the yacht glided through the water to the jetty...

Two spotlights flashed from the roof of the warehouse, and the beams of light crisscrossed the yacht. As the mercenaries leaped onto the jetty and ran for the building, automatic weapons fire screamed their way, muzzle flashes marking places of concealment. The mercs countered with their own small-arms fire, and the yacht crew returned fire with a Browning .50-cal machine gun mounted on the roof. The heavy-barreled weapon belched flame and spat lead at the flashing muzzles. The mercs at the front of the charge fired as they ran, but some fell as enemy bullets found their marks.

Stiletto's boots pounded on the jetty. Reaching the asphalt of the parking lot, he broke off from the rush and rolled to cover behind a stack of pallets. Two bullets smacked the pallets as he picked out a target and the M933 bucked against his shoulder. His target dived for cover.

The mercenaries fired from their positions, the crackles of gunfire mixed with yelling as squad leaders directed their teams.

Scott shifted onto his belly and began low-crawling with his eye on one corner of the warehouse.

A thought nagged at him.

This was an ambush.

The enemy had known they were coming.

It was probably too much of a stretch, Scott decided. More like they *expected* an attack and planned ahead.

So much for surprise. Darien Foster wasn't stupid. Was there *anything* of value in the warehouse?

The spotlights still blared, and a loud burst of .50-cal from the yacht shattered one. The other swept the lot, mercenaries rolling out of the way as enemy fire smacked those caught in the beam. Another blast from the yacht doused the remaining spotlight, and darkness descended on the battlefield.

Stiletto increased speed, the front of his black-suit dragging on the asphalt and his explosive-laden pack feeling like a turtle's shell. Sweat dripped into his eyes. His rapid heart rate wasn't because of the gunfire, but knowing he basically had a big bomb strapped to his back.

Bullets strafed the ground beside him, bits of asphalt stinging his cheeks. *Almost there.* Stiletto bolted to his feet and ran, firing in the general direction of the enemy. He reached the side of the warehouse, kicked open a door, and ran inside. His arrival surprised several enemy troopers positioned behind firing ports in the wall and he shot the closest two, stitching them from toe to head. Their bodies twitched and fell as the .223 slugs ripped into them, painting the warehouse wall a shade of sticky red. The remaining three shooters took off running, quickly getting lost in the maze of shelving and various crated items stacked floor to ceiling.

Stiletto spoke into the Motorola com link connecting him to Nikki. "I'm inside."

Nikki replied, "The firing has stopped, and we're moving in."

"You're welcome. Still three loose in the building, so be careful."

"Copy."

Stiletto stayed low behind some boxes and

tried to listen. The three gunmen had to communicate somehow. He couldn't hear any whispers over the ringing in his ears, though. They certainly weren't shouting, but they *were* somewhere.

Doors on the opposite side crashed inward, and there was shouting and firing. The sounds bounced off the walls and rose to a crescendo. Stray rounds nicked Scott's position, and he stayed flat to avoid behind hit by the enemy or his own guys.

The shooting stopped as if somebody had turned off a faucet. Stiletto listened on the com link as Nikki started shouting orders. Set up a perimeter. Get casualties back to the yacht. And then, "Scott, where are you?"

"Southwest corner."

"Come to the north wall. We found an office."

Stiletto ran down the aisle ahead of him and turned right when he reached the north wall. Midway down the walkway was indeed an office, where Nikki and two of the mercenaries were sorting papers and gathering a laptop and some portable hard drives.

Nikki stepped out as Scott approached.

"We must have caught them on an off-night," she said. "Half the force we expected."

"Nuts. They were waiting. Darien Foster put

everybody on alert, and we should have considered that."

One of the merc team leaders spoke over the com link about finding guns packed in the crates.

Nikki raised an eyebrow.

"We're not taking anything but the computers," Stiletto said.

Nikki told the mercs to forget the papers and take the laptops and hard drives. "Plant your bombs," she told Scott.

Stiletto unstrapped his bomb pack. Removing the weight made him feel better. He started with four thermite bombs as Nikki and her crew began clearing out, setting the bombs on the floor at the base of the walls on each side of the building.

A merc said over the com link, "Two trucks approaching fast."

Stiletto hurried with the C-4, which he placed at random among the crates and ran outside as the Browning .50 started firing on the new arrivals. Gunfire snapped from the mercs as they joined the hammering heavy machine gun. Return fire from the enemy as troops piled out of the trucks was drowned out by the thumping Browning. Relieved of the extra forty pounds of the bomb pack, Stiletto raced to the front line.

The two trucks sat askew on the east side of the parking lot, caught in a crossfire that didn't stop the enemy from shooting back. Rounds split the air as Stiletto dropped next to Nikki behind a stack of tires.

"We're wired," Stiletto reported.

Over the bursts of the .50-cal, Nikki Fortune ordered her men back to the yacht. Stiletto and Nikki provided covering fire as the mercenaries scrambled back to the boat, some carrying wounded. Salvos from the .50 struck one of the trucks, and the resulting explosion lit the night as a wave of heat washed over Scott. The neighboring truck ignited and blew, and the fireballs kept the enemy—those who survived—pinned down. The .50 stopped firing and the yacht's motors rumbled to life.

Stiletto took a remote detonator from a pocket of his blacksuit and looked back to see a line of mercs on the jetty.

Nikki said, "All clear," and took off for the yacht.

Stiletto ran after her. The .50 started again with thundering short burst as they turned their backs on the enemy. Once his boots hit the wooden jetty, Stiletto clamped a finger on the detonator button.

The warehouse collapsed like a house of cards. The walls buckled under the explosion first, then the roof caved in with a crash that echoed for miles. Secondary blasts sent trails of flame into the night sky. As the yacht left the jetty, chunks of flaming debris struck the deck and the water, but Nikki and the merc crew were already below.

Scott stayed on deck, kneeling at the stern and watching the fire. No night vision was required. The farther the yacht traveled, the more the fire looked as if it were consuming the entire island.

Taking a deep breath of the cold sea air, Stiletto rose. The first blow against the Foster alliance had been struck. How would Darien react? He slung the M933 over a shoulder and proceeded below.

He couldn't wait to get back on dry land.

He also couldn't wait to see what intel they had recovered.

CHAPTER 11

THE MERC CREW had been lucky—only ten wounded, no KIAs. The captured laptop and hard drives were brought to Nikki's spacious cabin, and Scott joined her to start sorting any information left on the computer.

Stiletto put the laptop in front of him on a small corner desk. Nikki stood over his shoulder.

"What do we do with anything we find?" she asked.

Stiletto pressed the Power button.

"We'll know when we find it."

The laptop was on in sleep mode and didn't have a password prompt. *Sloppy, guys*, he thought, but also typical. The bad guys could be as slack with security as the good guys, something Stiletto knew all too well.

He clicked on the Outlook folder and started reading email from Franko St. Regis to a man named Smolensky, whom Stiletto guessed was the fellow in charge of the now-destroyed warehouse operation. The exchanges resembled any regular business email communication, except they talked about moving guns and people and selling same.

The Greek police and Interpol would love the details.

Stiletto next found a warning sent by Darien Foster under that name about a potential raid. She knew Stiletto's name and a few details about him, especially his description, and stated that he was to be shot on sight. She did not want him as a prisoner.

Explains the ambush, he thought. If he gave the laptop to Suzi, she could back-trace where the notes had been sent from. Might be a lead there.

Scott and Nikki clicked around for two hours, and she brought in tea midway through. She disliked coffee as much as he did.

The emails were the only real clues. The rest of the hard drive contained shipping and receiving information and other notes made by Smolensky, whoever he was.

Finally, Stiletto pushed the laptop away.

"That was fun," she said. "Where do we go next?"

Stiletto, who was contemplating a bare wall in a daze, barely heard her. "Hmmm?"

Nikki leaned on the desk. "Where are we going next?"

"Let me sleep on it."

"That's a good idea." Nikki undid the top two buttons on her top and leaned forward to give Scott a peek at the valley between her breasts and the black bra snugly cupping them. He raised an eyebrow as she moved to his lap, but had no time to say no before she snaked an arm around his neck. She smelled of dried sweat and grit, and the feel of her soft bottom on his lap made him stir.

"Combat makes me horny, did I tell you?"

"You may have forgotten that detail."

She laughed. Her breath was hot against his neck.

"I suppose you need some relief then," he said, giving her a nudge. She slid off his lap to the floor, stretching out with her legs spread. Stiletto strad-dled her and began undoing the remaining buttons of her top while she bit her lower lip and looked him up and down with eager eyes.

Paris

A PRIVATE JET belonging to a Fortunado front company landed at Orly Airport in Paris under overcast skies.

After Customs officers checked their luggage, Scott and Nikki found a rental car desk and procured a sedan for five days. Stiletto wasn't sure how much time Suzi would need to trace the email messages on the laptop, but he figured a week was a good bet.

Stiletto drove away from the airport and dialed Suzi on his cell, holding the phone in front of his face so as not to take his eyes off the road.

Suzi answered on the first ring.

"You land yet?"

"Be there in twenty if traffic isn't too bad."

She laughed. "See you in an hour."

Stiletto put the phone back in his jacket and drove quietly with Nikki in the passenger seat beside him.

"Who is this woman?" she asked.

"She pretty much runs my life. You'll like her. She's a lot like you, except she works for herself. You ever consider that?"

"And do what?" Nikki inquired. "Start my own syndicate? You don't realize the advantage my father gives me."

"I guess I was always eager to get away from my folks," Stiletto said. "When the time came, I took the opportunity."

"Why did you want to leave so bad?"

"Army brat. Got tired of moving around all the time."

"Um, I hate to tell you—"

"I know." He smiled. "The irony is not lost on me. Or my family."

Nikki had opened her mouth to respond when Stiletto's cell phone rang. He pulled out the phone expecting to see Suzi's name on the caller ID, but that was not the case. The number displayed meant nothing to him. Paris area code, though.

He answered as traffic slowed. "Who is this?"

"Hello, Mr. Scott Stiletto."

A chill raced up Scott's back. "Hello, Darien."

Nikki's eyes widened and she looked at Stiletto intently.

"You don't sound very surprised," Darien commented.

"Not after last night. Sorry about the warehouse we blew up."

"Makes no difference to me. We'll build another. But here's the thing. You may think you know all about me, but there's a lot I know about you, too. And the people close to you. See ya!"

Stiletto pulled the phone away from his ear like it was hot and cleared the screen.

"What did she say?" Nikki said.

Stiletto ignored her and dialed Suzi, cutting her off before she finished saying hello. "Suzi, take precautions. I have a feeling you're about to be attacked."

"What?"

"Get out your guns, and I'll be there ASAP."

Suzi cursed and hung up.

Stiletto wove around a few cars to get ahead, but a traffic light stopped him. He updated Nikki, and she took a pistol from her purse and checked the load.

"We have plenty of people here if it gets too hot," she said, stowing the gun under her left leg.

"I knew there was a reason I brought you along."

The light changed, and Stiletto stepped on the accelerator.

Suzi Weber rolled her wheelchair away from the desk.

Her trio of monitors and a set of cell phones occupied the desk, her tools of the trade.

In her former life, Suzi had been an analyst for the CIA working with a team in Iraq. A small grocery store had been their cover, the store up front, agency personnel in the rear. Insurgents had found the hideout thanks to sloppy security by their team leader and crashed a truckload of explosives through the grocery, setting off his bombs before the vehicle stopped moving.

Six of her colleagues had died. She'd been lucky.

Sort of.

Now she sold her collection, analysis, and team coordination skills on the free market to clients like Stiletto who were always on the move and needed somebody securely in one place to handle daily incidentals.

She'd been a looker once, with long legs and an athletic physique. Those long legs were useless now, and she'd grown a little thick in the middle because all she did was sit. Upper body exercises helped somewhat.

The "saddlebags" on either side of the chair held other tools. Another cell phone on the left, and a Beretta 92 on the right, the pistol loaded with +P hollow-points for maximum power and flesh-shredding capabilities.

She wheeled across the room. She had a street-level one bedroom apartment with a couch in front of the tv in the corner opposite her desk. She could get onto the couch and back into the chair easily enough, but any other furniture was a hazard she didn't need. Suzi grunted with effort as she hooked a left into the kitchen, where she rotated to face the front door. The position also gave her a view of the windows looking out on the street. The windows were curtained inside and barred outside, but a skilled gun crew could blast off the bars with a little C-4 easily enough.

Suzi removed the Beretta from the right-side pocket and jacked back the slide to chamber a round. She breathed a little faster than normal, eyes snapping from window to door.

An engine rumbled out front, the vehicle stopping on the street. She tried to see through the curtain. It was too soon to be Scott. Doors opened and closed, and the engine kept running.

Suzi took a deep breath and slowly let it out. Two hard bangs shook her door, and then it crashed open and two men armed with silenced automatics raced through it. With no furniture for cover, they were caught in the open and Suzi opened fire from behind the counter. Three fast rounds from the Beretta knocked back one of the gunmen and he crashed to the beige carpet. The other raised his weapon, but the Beretta popped three more times. The killer took each bullet high in the chest but only fell to his knees, a stunned expression on his acne-scarred face. After a moment, he fell onto his stomach and fired once. The shot smacked into a copper pot hanging on the wall behind her, and the resulting clang filled the room.

The gunman grunted and started dragging himself across the carpet, a snail's trail of red gore in his wake. Suzi threw her weight forward, landing hard on the carpet, the chair rolling back. She aimed around the corner of the counter, and the gunman took too long to react. One shot from the Beretta popped his left eye like a bubble and exploded out the back of his head. The gunman flopped, lay flat, and no longer moved.

Suzi let out a breath and rolled onto her back to see where the chair was, then rolled back onto her belly. She slid on the tiled floor to the chair, clamping a brake on one wheel while she grasped the armrests and started lifting herself off the floor.

Voices from the hall. "Suzi!"

Scott!

"In here!"

She was halfway back in the chair when his reassuring grip lifted her off the ground. She dropped into the seat.

"What are you doing out of the chair?" he asked.

"You try having a gunfight in one of these and get back to me. Who the hell is she?"

A tall, dark-haired woman with a pistol stood behind Scott, watching the door.

"I'm Nikki," she said.

"You brought her with you?" Suzi asked Scott.

"Try working an op alone and get back to me."

"We need to scoot," Nikki told them.

Suzi said, "My getaway pack is in the hall closet."

Stiletto left to get it.

Suzi told Nikki, "Go to my desk and look for a box with a button."

Nikki found the box. "Should I press it?"

"Yes."

The box, basically an external drive, would send a virus into her computers and make the machines useless. She stored everything on the cloud, so the data was easily restored.

Nikki eyed the computers with a frown. They appeared to have not changed status, hard drives humming and screens blank. "What's supposed to happen?"

"It's already happening."

Stiletto returned with Suzi's case and set it in her lap, then moved behind the chair and pushed.

"One of these days," he said, "the cops will be right around the corner and we'll have a lot of explaining to do."

"Shut up and push," Suzi ordered.

Nikki's local contacts provided a hotel suite overlooking the Eiffel Tower. Stiletto stood on the deck, puffing on a Montecristo and taking in the sight.

"You look like you've never seen it before,"

Nikki said. She stopped beside him. "Your girl-friend has thrown me out."

"That's why I'm on the deck," Stiletto explained.

Suzi occupied the suite's dining table with her laptop as well as the computer Stiletto had captured in Greece, running a program to trace the origin points of Darien Foster's emails. He didn't know how such equipment and software worked, but he knew she could put the connections together and provide another lead.

"Did you call your family?" Nikki asked.

"Yes," Scott told her. The exchange with Darien Foster had two meanings as far as he was concerned, and after getting Suzi out of danger, he'd phoned his father and brother to warn them of the potential threat. He didn't think Darien wanted to target them. The expense wasn't justi-fied, and he hoped they might keep their fight "pro-fessional," as ridiculous as that sounded, but he didn't want to take the chance.

"I'd really like a shot at St. Regis," Stiletto said. "If we can isolate Foster, she'll start making mistakes."

"Don't bet on it. She has connections everywhere, and she's been on her own for a long time, before St. Regis. It won't be that easy."

"Just once it would be nice to have it easy."

Suzi called them inside. Scott left his cigar on the rail, and he and Nikki joined Suzi at the dining table. The laptop monitor showed a map of the globe with green and red dots on the West Coast of the US and throughout Europe.

"Foster is on the move," Suzi explained, "and these red dots represent where she's been. Her emails were sent from those spots, from her mobile phone. Look at the flurry prior to leaving the US, and then only two more once she reached Europe. And the dots are pointing north."

"But there was only one note sent to the warehouse," Nikki said.

"She was warning everybody using separate notes instead of a mass mailing," Stiletto said. "Also, she might be lining up clients to buy the Jordan Corp. data."

"Right, but now look at the green dots," Suzi said. "Those are St. Regis. You can see he's moved around a little, but most of his emails originate from Stuttgart."

Suzi zoomed on Stuttgart. Stiletto didn't recognize what part of the city the dots were in, but it was enough to make him want to get on a plane and find Foster's partner in crime.

"Can you get an address?" Stiletto asked.

"Already running a script for that," Suzi said. "Should have something in a few hours. Who's buying lunch?"

Stuttgart, Germany

FRANKO ST. REGIS absently rubbed the mole on his chin as he listened to Rafe Smolensky talk about the number of items and amount of money that were lost in the attack on the warehouse.

After Darien communicated to them that Stiletto was on the warpath, Smolensky had made the defensive arrangements and directed the ambush from a safe point. He hadn't expected an army, he explained to St. Regis. All they had on Stiletto suggested he'd either come alone or only use two or three men in support. Twenty soldiers and a yacht with a heavy machine gun hadn't factored into Smolensky's defense plan.

"Who is helping him?" St. Regis asked. "Who is financing him? A force that size is not cheap."

"He's rumored to have visited the Fortunados in Sicily," Smolensky said.

St. Regis raised an eyebrow. "What did he promise them other than revenge?"

Smolensky shrugged. He was a slight man with scars on his face from, of all things, a drunk-driving accident where the driver had struck his car and he, not wearing his seatbelt, had gone through the windshield. He'd been lucky to survive.

"We didn't count on the Fortunados," Smolensky said. "Shall we send a team to kill them?"

St. Regis shook his head. "That won't help until after we take care of Stiletto."

Music and thumping bass drifted up through the floor. St. Regis' office was above a downtown beer hall, and he directed the syndicate's operations from his small space on the second floor.

"We probably shouldn't stay here," Smolensky warned him.

"The warehouse was one thing, but they won't pull something like that in public," St. Regis said.

For once St. Regis was glad his office had no windows.

"What I want downstairs," St. Regis said, "is more men."

"We can't stay here all the time."

"Of course not. Make sure the crew is ready to travel. I'll have a safe house prepared that isn't known to Darien. That may help a little."

Smolensky nodded and left the office.

St. Regis stared at his cluttered desktop and wondered what to do. Darien had diverted too many troops for her planned sale for them to have anybody capable of tracking Stiletto before he reached them. The Fortunados knew too much.

Staying alive would be up to him and the few gunners he had close by.

Stiletto and Nikki landed in Stuttgart in the middle of the afternoon.

"Do you have any contacts here?" he asked as he drove away from the airport in a rented BMW.

"Not directly," she said. "My father can ask a favor of one or two people should we require."

"Let's go see this bar first." Stiletto steered the car through traffic. The city reminded him of DC— a lot of cars jammed together in not enough road space.

They eventually found the beer hall on Guten-bergstradt, with other restaurants and shops along the street. The other establishments gave Stiletto an idea.

"Give me ten minutes, then go pull a fire alarm in one of these places."

"Are you nuts?"

"No. When you've done that, get back in the car and keep the motor running."

He opened the door to get out.

"What are you going to do?" Nikki said.

Stiletto winked at her. "Have a drink."

He left the car and started across the street. He didn't want to risk a gunfight in a crowded place or on a packed street. He'd been in enough of those to know that the chance of a civilian getting hurt was too great, and he didn't want to miss the opportunity to get St. Regis *now*. He had to know where Darien was, and Scott meant to pry that information out of St. Regis' head one way or another.

He heard the music inside the beer hall before stepping through the doorway. Once inside, the real assault on his ears began. Luckily it was a live band on a small stage at the back of the hall, and they worked out the nights' music set in short bursts.

There weren't many customers, but the ones that sat at tables had hard faces and didn't talk much to their companions. They also barely touched their beers.

Soldiers, and no mistake. As he eased onto a barstool, Scott decided his fire alarm plan wasn't such a bad idea. The goons wouldn't want a fight in public any more than he did. He wanted to work the distraction of emergency crews to his full advantage.

The bartender asked for his order and Stiletto said, "Tell St. Regis that Scott Stiletto is here."

"Who?"

"Your boss. The man upstairs. And I don't mean Jesus Christ." Stiletto opened his coat to show the butt of the Colt. "Tell him."

The bartender leaned forward. "Look around. You won't last two seconds."

"Nobody's doing any shooting today, Fritz. Tomorrow, maybe. Call St. Regis."

The bartender scowled and reached for a telephone under the counter. After some rapid-fire German, he hung up. "He'll be down."

Stiletto put money on the bar and asked for a Maker's and Coke. "Pour it so I can watch."

The bartender put a bottle and can of Coke in front of Scott with a curse.

"And a glass?"

The bartender slammed down the glass so hard Scott was surprised it didn't break.

Scott had poured and had taken two sips when Franko St. Regis sat down on the neighboring stool.

"You are a brave man, Mr. Stiletto."

"If by brave you mean stupid."

"I might. You're surrounded."

"So?"

"There's nobody else here with you."

"Isn't there?"

St. Regis sighed. "What do you want?"

"Peace and quiet."

"Something not impossible to provide."

"Where's Darien?"

"What did I say about impossible?"

Stiletto swallowed more of his drink. "Why don't you do the right thing and tell me where she is? You know deep down that she'll cut you out eventually. Why not save yourself and enjoy the reward?"

"What reward?"

"Jordan Corp. is offering two million US," Stiletto informed him.

"The plans are worth way more than that."

"But this way you get to live and enjoy the money."

St. Regis frowned but didn't respond right away. Stiletto didn't break eye-contact. He wondered what Kim Jordan would say if he asked her for the two million.

St. Regis asked, "What if I say no?"

Stiletto shrugged. "Then we go back to Plan A."

"Which is what?"

"Kill you and go to the next link in the chain." Stiletto downed the rest of his drink. "It really doesn't matter to me who gets the reward. Somebody in your organization will bite. Maybe Smolensky?"

Stiletto checked his watch.

"You have two minutes, and then we do this the hard way."

"I said you were surrounded," St. Regis said. "You aren't suicidal."

"Minute and a half."

"What promises do I have that you won't betray me?"

"If you know my record at all, you also know I'm a straight shooter. Sixty seconds."

St. Regis tapped the mole on his chin. *Must be his thinking gesture*, Scott mused, although he figured anybody else would want the thing lopped off.

"I don't think I believe you," St. Regis said.

"Okay."

The band stopped momentarily, the musicians conferring over an arrangement, and a shrill bell sounded from somewhere.

"Sounds like the fire alarm next door," Stiletto said.

"What have you started?"

"Nothing. I'm alone, remember?"

The sirens outside meant police and fire arriving to check the alarm. The goons stirred, primed for orders, casting anxious glances at St. Regis' back.

Stiletto took out the .45 and jammed the muzzle into Franko's gut.

"Tell them to stand down. We're going outside."

"They'll kill you."

"You'll die too, and that won't do you any good. Give the order, and we'll take a nice drive."

Stiletto jabbed him with the .45 for extra emphasis and St. Regis winced.

CHAPTER 12

Two POLICE UNITS and one fire truck blocked the lane in front of the beer hall and the next-door beauty shop as Stiletto escorted St. Regis across the street to where Nikki waited in the BMW.

He shoved St. Regis into the back seat but didn't put away his automatic. Nikki eased into traffic, and presently they cleared the congestion. Nikki turned north.

"My men will follow," St. Regis told them.

Stiletto laughed quietly and asked Nikki, "Where are we going?"

"I asked for one of those favors while you were relaxing at the bar," she replied. "It will be nice and quiet. Hi, Franko."

"Ms. Fortunado."

"Call off the goons and make a deal," Stiletto suggested. "You can't trust Darien, and deep down you know that."

"You have grossly overestimated yourself."

"Why? You two married?"

St. Regis laughed. "No, but she and I have a special understanding."

"I have no idea what that means," Stiletto said.

RAFE SMOLENSKY hurriedly gathered three volunteer gunmen and piled them into a vehicle, which he drove away from the beer hall in the same direction as the BMW.

He did not want a second defeat on his back. If he could rescue Franko, maybe Darien wouldn't have him killed.

NIKKI FOLLOWED AM KRAHERWALD, houses on one side and forest on the other, until she slowed for a right turn into a side road that ended in a small parking lot. There were no other cars, and no sign of any activity. They were at a soccer field overseen by empty bleachers, with a small shack near the seats.

Stiletto asked no questions as he ordered a now-nervous Franko St. Regus out of the BMW.

"Follow me," Nikki said.

Stiletto urged St. Regis forward with another jab from the .45, and the man turned to glare at Scott before following Nikki.

"No sign of your rescue squad yet, huh?"

St. Regis looked back again with narrowed eyes. Nikki pulled on the door of the shack, which was storage for yard equipment. Stiletto shoved St. Regis hard in the back and sent him tumbling into the shed, where he landed face-first on the dusty wood floor.

St. Regis rose to his hands and knees and cast furtive glances at the lawn equipment. All of the items were clamped to the walls.

"Won't be that easy, Franko. Turn over and sit down."

St. Regis complied, keeping his hands planted behind his back for support.

"What makes you think I'll talk here rather than at the bar?" he asked.

Stiletto raised an eyebrow at Nikki.

She said, "Who says we want you to talk? This is a nice place to shoot you, and then my friends will come by and clean up."

"You can still get the reward, Franko."

St. Regis opened his mouth wide to scream. "There is no reward! Stop talking and shoot!"

A car engine revved behind them, scattered small arms fire popping, and Nikki yelled and ran for the BMW. St. Regis tried to kick the .45 out of Scott's hand, but Stiletto easily dodged and then shot St. Regis. At such close range, the bullet smashed through St. Regis' head and split open the lower part of his face. He fell flat on the shed floor.

Stiletto pivoted to face the new threat. St. Regis' buddies were a day late and a dollar short.

Nikki Fortune was already kneeling by the front of the BMW with a stubby submachine gun in both hands. Her salvo cut across the hood and part of the windshield. The car rocked to a stop, the doors flew open, and four gunners piled out. Stiletto tracked the driver, a man with scars on his face, and knocked him down with a double-tap to the chest. He rolled right, avoiding return fire that kicked up dirt and shredded the shed's doorway.

The gunmen who exited behind Scarface fired as he ran for the trees on the edge of the field. Stiletto fired twice but missed, the gunman reaching cover. Scott shouted for Nikki to move as he advanced on the shooter, firing once, the gunman recoiling as bits of tree bark struck him in the face. Stiletto fired again and blood burst from the gunner's neck, spraying outward as the man collapsed.

More submachine gun chatter came from Nikki as Stiletto reloaded the .45 and ran for the BMW. The gunmen had taken cover at the rear of their car, the final two squatting by the bumper. Stiletto stopped and steadied his aim, and his first round took off the head of the gunner nearest. The other screamed as chunks of his friend landed on him, and he broke cover enough for a burst from Nikki to catch him in the chest. The shooter fell back.

Stiletto ran to Scarface and patted his pockets, finding a cell phone. Nikki turned the BMW around and started for the exit, Stiletto jumping into the passenger seat as the car moved. Nikki mashed the accelerator to the floor to get the car out of there.

"This is getting expensive," she said.

"Why?"

"I promised my friends one body, not five."

. . .

STILETTO FIDDLED with the cell phone he had taken from Scarface.

"What are you going to do with that?" Nikki asked.

"Call Darien and gloat."

The phone started to ring.

"That was fast," Nikki said. "Is it her?"

Stiletto grinned.

"Yup," Stiletto answered. "Hello, Darien."

Silence on the line a moment, then, "I figured. When I heard you'd taken Franko—"

"Franko's dead, and you're next unless you want to hand over the data."

Darien Foster laughed. "All you've done is thin the herd! Now there are fewer people to demand a share of my money when I sell your precious data."

"You won't live long enough to sell anything, hon."

"Let's test your theory. I'm holding an auction in Ireland at the Ashbrook Castle. We've reserved the whole building. It's out in the country—great place for a last stand. Come to the belly of the beast, and then we'll see who comes out on top."

"We already know how this is going to end, Darien."

"Oh, I'm sure there's still a surprise or two waiting for one of us."

Stiletto killed the connection and told Nikki.

"That woman has some balls," she admitted.

"Where are we going?" he said.

"A hotel. Remember what I said about combat?"

"No."

"Yes!"

"No, Nikki."

"All work and no play, et cetera."

Stiletto shook his head. It was a hard life. "All right, but you're gonna do what *I* tell you this time."

She cracked an evil grin and ran a hand up his left leg to squeeze his crotch. "Yes, Master."

And she did.

ALL WAS QUIET.

Darien Foster knew the tranquility wouldn't last long.

She surveyed the Ashbrook Castle from a grassy hill almost fifty yards away. The ancient castle had long ago been converted into a very pricey tourist spot, and she'd rented the entire building for her auction.

The stone castle sat in the middle of a field of green grass, clusters of trees at the rear and a creek running through the wooded area. The rest of the surrounding land was also a glorious green with rolling hills, and the clear blue sky made the environment absolutely breathtaking.

"Where do you want the patrols?"

The question came from the buzz-cut blond man next to her named Ross, one of her soldiers.

"This fifty-yard radius will be fine," she told him.

She had no illusions that the auction would go without incident. Any of her guests might try to pull a fast one, and Stiletto and the Fortunado woman would for sure try something.

And then there was Emil Karga to contend with.

She had a team running around the world looking for the Russian, but he'd managed to cover his tracks well. No sign of him even at his hideout in the Balkans, which meant he was still on the move and probably searching for her just as earnestly.

Word of the auction had gone out in the underground whisper stream by now. If Karga had a chance to organize a gun crew, he'd show up one way or another.

"I'll get the squads organized," Ross said.

"I'm going to stay out for a while."

Ross said okay and began walking back to the castle.

When Darien had told Ross about challenging Stiletto to show up, he had disagreed. Yes, it was risky, but she wanted Stiletto and the woman to face her men in an arena of her own design, where they'd be outnumbered and, best of all, outgunned. There'd be no escape for either. She was smarter than St. Regis and Smolensky and would not make their mistakes. She'd faced Stiletto already, and the American had no chance. Her pride demanded she kill him personally. She planned to send pieces of the Fortunado woman back to her father, starting with a finger or an ear.

As for Karga. . .

She had a gruesome end in mind for that Russian swine.

Stiletto studied pictures of the castle on his

cell phone as Nikki drove along the winding two-lane road.

Every now and then he looked out at the lush green countryside, but the impending violence was never far from his thoughts. He wanted to smell the roses while keeping the thorns in mind.

At least they were in the Republic and not forced to reckon with stray IRA activity in the North. But it was the Republic where Stiletto felt slightly off-kilter. His maternal grandfather had fought for Irish independence against the British alongside Michael Collins at the post office in 1917. He'd fled to America rather than take part in the Irish Civil War that followed the victory, as he refused to kill his own countrymen. He'd died hoping to see Ireland united again, but Stiletto wasn't sure that was possible even in his lifetime.

Scott set his mind back on the castle. The structure impressed him, but the flat surroundings did not. The trees and creek behind the castle offered very little in terms of cover or an escape route. The land, despite its rolling hills, meant anybody fighting was doing so out in the open and fully exposed.

It was the perfect way to discourage an assault,

really, but there was one problem. Darien's people would be exposed too.

The best way to attack the place would be from the air, and if a force didn't have air support, then a rocket or mortar attack provided a similar advantage.

"What do you think?" Nikki said.

"A lot of things," Stiletto said absently. He provided a rundown of his observations.

He had to admit that Nikki Fortune was an asset. She'd really smoothed their Paris and Stuttgart visits with her various contacts, and the warehouse raid off Greece had been particularly valuable.

Stiletto still didn't trust her, though. Helping him if she wanted the anti-stealth data for herself helped *her*, too.

Stiletto put away his phone. The road straightened for a short stretch before a new series of curves began. The pavement was very smooth, obviously not heavily traveled, and they'd seen no other vehicles since reaching the countryside.

"Awfully lonely out here," Nikki remarked. "Not even any farms or animals. Nothing."

"We'll have plenty of company soon enough," Stiletto stated.

. . .

THEY WERE the third car in line at the arched entrance of the castle. A short wall extended from either side of the arch but did not go all the way around the building. At one time, Stiletto thought, it probably had. At either end of the wall, tall bushes grew instead.

Two armed guards, both thin with muscles showing through their tight clothes, manned the gate. One checked invitations while the other observed, both toting automatic rifles with pistols on their belts.

When Nikki pulled up at the gate, the guard on her side said, "Invitation."

"We have a verbal invite," Stiletto said. "Ask your boss. Stiletto and Fortune."

The guard removed a folded piece of paper from his front shirt pocket and read down the page.

"Okay," he said, waving them on. Nikki drove through the gate and parked the car in the line of other vehicles to the left of the gate. Scott decided they could easily drive across the grass to the main road thirty yards away should the need arise.

Stiletto and Nikki exited the car, collected luggage from the trunk, one case each, and walked across the grass to the front steps at the castle's entrance.

The open doors loomed like the mouth of a hungry lion, and Stiletto suddenly doubted the wisdom of walking into such an obvious no-win situation.

CHAPTER 13

A YOUNG REDHEADED woman in a suit with a short skirt escorted Scott and Nikki to their third-floor room and said, "Dinner is at six, and the auction starts at eight." She left, and the door shut quietly behind her.

"Nice room," Nikki said. She placed her suitcase on the bed, opened it, and dug through clothes to pull out a device the size of a pack of cigarettes. She flicked a switch and moved around the room. The box beeped several times, revealing listening devices in the nightstand lamp and behind two paintings.

"Typical," Stiletto said.

Nikki put the bug detector back in the suitcase. Stiletto admired how her jeans stretched over her

BRIAN DRAKE

plump rear end and went over to smack her bottom. Nikki spun on him with fiery eyes and he grabbed her and pulled her close, her body hot to the touch.

"Let's give the eavesdroppers something to listen to," he suggested.

They did.

STILETTO LAUGHED as he buttered a piece of bread.

"What's so funny?" Nikki asked, about to take a sip from a glass of wine.

"With all the faces I'm seeing, we could clear up a ton of old CIA cases."

The crowd in the wide and high-ceilinged dining room ran the gamut of the Agency's Most Wanted. A Vietnamese crime lord. A French gun-runner. A Swedish computer hacker. Variety of known terrorists, from the German Red Brigade to Japanese Red Army to holdouts from al-Qaeda, all of them well-dressed and enjoying beef or chicken in an ornate dining room complete with crystal chandeliers, white linen tablecloths, and soft piano music courtesy of the redhead who had checked them in. She sat in front of the keys, playing without a songbook.

Stiletto and Nikki both had the tri-tip, which was perfectly cooked. Neither expected the meal to be poisoned since the plates had come off a large tray carried by the servers, who asked each guest want they wanted. If Darien wanted them dead in that fashion, she'd have to be clairvoyant.

Scott felt a little out of place at their table, jammed into a corner, only the two of them. Some of the other guests occasionally glanced their way, probably wondering why the two of them were special enough not to have to share with anybody else while they had to sit with company many would have preferred not to socialize with.

Stiletto consoled himself by pointing out that soon it wouldn't matter, although he was still working on a plan. He wondered if Darien inviting them here wasn't so much to put them in a trap as mock them. If she could turn the crowd against them, they'd be outgunned with no hope of escape.

No sign of Darien Foster yet, but she'd arrive soon. He had no doubt.

THE REDHEAD CEASED PLAYING the piano once

the dishes had been collected and called for everybody's attention. She told them she was Ava Courtney, and that she would be Ms. Foster's representative during the auction.

Stiletto frowned. Where had Darien gone?

Ava Courtney drew back a curtain on the wall behind her to reveal a large flat-screen monitor that showed Darien's face.

"Thank you for coming, everybody," Darien said into the camera. "I hope you understand my need to take precautions with the item for sale."

Muffled laughs all around.

She didn't say she's not in the castle, Stiletto noted.

Darien said, "My assistant Ava will show you what you are bidding on and answer all questions. I will see you all, and the winner, very soon. Good luck."

Darien Foster vanished from the screen, replaced by a schematic of a radar dish.

"There it is," Stiletto said.

"But where is she?"

"Somewhere. Only a matter of finding her."

Ava Courtney began a short lesson on how the anti-stealth radar system worked and explained some of the science behind the design.

"What do we do?" Nikki said.

"*We* do nothing. *You* stay here and come get me if I'm not back in a reasonable amount of time."

Nikki Fortune didn't argue as Scott left the table.

He ignored the looks of the guards as he moved through the dining room. They wore suits and did not display rifles, but undoubtedly carried pistols under their dinner jackets.

Scott turned a corner, heading for the men's room off the lobby, but instead continued past and through a stairwell door.

He paused on the landing, easing the door shut. He didn't think Darien was on the upper floors, although the possibility existed. The background behind her had been obscured by a black curtain, but she'd want to be close to the main floor in case she required a quick exit, and a side door in the basement leading outside probably fit the bill.

Stiletto started down the steps.

Emil Karga mentally cursed Darien up one side and down the other.

Karga lay on the grass, propped on his elbows, a pair of binoculars at his eyes. His team was in a line to his left, metal clanking as they set up a mortar. Karga condemned her while at the same time commending her ingenuity at selecting such a site for her auction. He couldn't be positive he'd have done the same. It was a shame he needed to kill her.

For his own position, Karga had selected the highest hill, which wasn't saying much, and he felt the prickly grass beneath him even through his combat fatigues.

He counted the guards outside and noted the passing of a three-man patrol team who didn't venture beyond a fifty-yard line. He and his crew were about two hundred yards from the castle, and the patrol was too far away to notice them or their Land Rover another hundred yards back.

The big question on his mind was where to bomb first. The line of parked cars, sure. But where in the castle was everybody gathered?

A hand touched his left shoulder. Karga pulled away the binoculars and turned his head.

"We're set."

Killkin's replacement, a short and wiry Russkie named Simokoff, had said the words.

Karga nodded and spoke past Simokoff to the three men behind him, who were assembling and loading sniper rifles. He told them to set up on the hill and wait for the patrol. Simokoff, he put in charge of the mortar. A case of high-explosive projectiles sat near the tall tube.

Karga rolled onto his right side and flashed a hand signal to the driver of the Land Rover. When the time came, they'd take the vehicle to the burning castle and go find Darien.

Unlike Ms. Foster, who needed the auction to sell the Jordan Corp. data, Karga already had a buyer lined up, and his buyer still expected delivery. Emil Karga intended to meet his commitment to the deal.

And he'd made it clear to his men: Darien Foster was not to survive the night.

For Stiletto, he had other plans. Connections in Moscow had communicated to him that they'd love to have Stiletto answer for crimes he'd recently committed in the Motherland. Karga knew a little about them but was more interested in the money he'd receive for delivering the American. It would be a magnificent night where he'd get rid of two enemies at the same time.

. . .

"WHAT ARE YOU DOING WANDERING AROUND?" the guard asked.

Stiletto had taken no more than two steps away from the stairway when the trooper spotted him. The man wore a custom-fitted tan suit and what were undoubtedly steel-toed shoes that were perfectly polished.

Stiletto was particularly interested in the man's submachine gun.

"Looking for the toilet, relax," Scott said. "You guys a little high-strung or what?"

"We put signs up."

"Well, it's a nice castle, and I got a little side-tracked. What's your problem?"

"Go back to the auction."

"May I pee first?"

"You can hold it." The guard raised the SMG's muzzle to Stiletto's midsection. "I catch you snooping again, and you won't have to worry about a piss ever again."

"You talk too much."

The man stepped forward, anger clouding his face. "What?"

Stiletto pivoted on his left foot and snapped his right leg up and out. The heel of his shoe struck the guard square on the chin, slamming back his head, and the guard fell to the hardwood floor with a finality that suggested he wasn't getting up again. Stiletto didn't stop to check and instead unslung the man's SMG, putting a pair of extra magazines in a pocket.

He looked around. Long hallway. Concrete floor and walls with high bulbs dangling from the ceiling, each one swaying a little. The swaying bulbs made deep shadows of doorways and alcoves and Stiletto froze in place, trying to stretch his hearing to listen for any other sounds.

He heard nothing. Instead, the basement felt like a tomb, and he was alive inside.

THE DREARY BASEMENT was the last place in which Darien Foster wanted to spend time, but security required she be apart from the main auction. She sat in one of the basement rooms that had been set up for the night with food, beverages, a large-screen television monitor, and decent lighting. She'd have liked a throw rug or something on the walls. Gray concrete bored her. But as she watched redheaded Ava Courtney give her nerdy science lecture and toggled the camera shots to examine the faces of her guests, she thought less of her surroundings and more of how much the sale would bring.

Some of her guests looked bored, checking their cell phones like any other mind-numbed dope, while others paid close attention with a gleam in their eyes. They saw value in what Ava Courtney described. They wanted the design data

Some of her guests were obviously there as proxy representatives of governments who wanted an edge on the US. She figured they'd be the heavy bidders. The others would probably buy and re-sell. She didn't think a garden-variety criminal had the ability or patience to actually build the radar system.

A radio crackled behind her and Ross responded. The patrol was checking in once again, all well. Ross paced behind Darien, his heavy foot-falls part of the video soundtrack.

Darien used her remote to switch back to the camera focused on Ava. The redhead was wrap-ping up her presentation. Darien clicked through the angles once again and froze on the shot of Scott Stiletto's table, from which Stiletto was now miss-ing. The Fortunado woman sat alone looking anxious.

Darien started to say something but cut her

words short as the door swung open on squeaky hinges.

STILETTO STARTED FORWARD, a quick glance behind him showing no threats. The palms of his hands sweated on the SMG, and he avoided the dangling lights by staying close to the right-hand wall. The concrete floor was indeed solid, but it felt like every step might land on an explosive mine that would send him into oblivion.

The bulbs pierced the darkness ahead, but every dark doorway made him pause.

Finally, a doorway on the left-side wall showed a crack of light under the bottom edge. He stopped across from the door, wiping both hands on his pants, and listened again.

The science lecture was loud and clear.

Confident resolve replaced nervousness as Stiletto approached the door, carefully turned the knob, and gave the door a shove. The hinges whined as the door swung open, the weight of the wood carrying it all the way, and there was Darien Foster sitting before a large-screen television with a camera mounted on top. The black curtain hung between two metal rods behind her. Her head was turned his direction, her eyes wide and unblinking.

Stiletto lifted the SMG to his shoulder and advanced through the doorway.

"Hands up, Darien."

She muted the tv, put the remote in her lap, and lifted her hands.

"Where's the thumb drive?"

"You fool," she said. "Do you think I'm stupid enough to have it here?"

A flurry of movement on his right took Stiletto's eyes from Darien long enough to see a crew-cut blond man coming around the curtain. Stiletto tried to turn the SMG on him, but the man struck with a low kick to Scott's midsection. His breath left him, and after he doubled over, more hard blows landed on his back. He dropped to the ground, and his ribs took a blow from a steel-toed boot. The SMG left his grip next, kicked away, and he rolled onto his side, curling up, pain flooding his body. Another kick. And another.

"Don't kill him, Ross."

Scott felt her hands on his body, and she pulled the Colt from his shoulder rig.

"Put him in the chair."

Strong hands lifted him from the floor and

dropped Stiletto in the chair. He sucked air in short gasps, eyes watery, but he met Darien's gaze when she stood before him. She held the .45 casually and had already clicked off the safety.

"You think you're smart, don't you?"

"Right now," Stiletto rasped, "I'm quite sore."

"You also think you're a comedian."

"It's a hobby." Stiletto shifted, stifling a groan. "I'll feel this in the morning."

"What's the plan with your girlfriend?" Darien picked up the remote and switched the monitor to Stiletto's table. Nikki Fortune sat with her arms folded and her lips pressed together.

"How long is she supposed to wait?" Darien asked.

"If she's still sitting there, maybe she has a reason."

"Maybe she wants to bid."

"I've actually considered that."

Darien laughed. "Do you even know why I'm doing this?"

"The obvious answer is money, but it's what you'll do with the money that gives the true answer."

"Right. The proceeds will finance my revenge against the Russian scum who murdered my parents. They still live like fat cats, fully protected. And thanks to you, I don't have to split the money with St. Regis or Smolensky."

"I know a little about revenge," Stiletto said. "I also know you're left with shattered dreams and spend the rest of your life trying to pick up the pieces."

"I don't care," Darien said.

CHAPTER 14

Nikki Fortune sat with folded arms, lips pressed together, her body a tight coil of energy looking for an outlet.

The guards in the room were riled about something. There were more now, and lots of whispered conferring, and one of them stood against the wall mere feet from her table. The activity could only mean something had happened to Scott, and she was well past the point at which she'd agreed to go looking for him.

She looked around as bidding started off at half a million dollars. The guests responded with enthusiasm.

Nikki needed a diversion, but what?

The building shook with a tremendous blast,

followed by another, and the third explosion shattered the windows of the dining hall, a rush of heat and sharp debris flying into the room. Nikki dived under the table as knife-edged shards of glass landed around her.

She pulled her pistol from concealment.

Be careful what you wish for.

EMIL KARGA GAVE the order as the three-man patrol rounded the castle and proceeded into view.

His sniper team fired as one, the suppressor-fitted Dragunov SVDs thumping their 7.62x54r flesh-shredders straight at the patrol. The bullets screamed across the field as Karga watched the patrol through the binoculars, and all three fell to impacts in their necks or heads.

"Target the cars first," Karga told Simokoff.

Karga's number two dropped the first mortar into the LLR 81mm tube. The five-foot tube extended well above the top of the hill but provided excellent aiming capability. The explosive projectile left the tube with a puff of smoke, and within seconds, one of the parked cars exploded, lighting up the night with orange flame. Karga felt the ground rumble underneath him. The first blast ignited other cars on either side, the blasts lifting the cars a few feet off the ground before dropping them back to earth.

Karga said, "Building."

Simokoff dropped one and then another projectile into the mortar tube. The first round hit the upper level of the castle, sending chunks of concrete and rebar onto the grass. The next 81mm landed near a row of lighted windows, the explosion blasting out the glass and the resulting fire spreading up the inside wall.

"Again," Karga ordered.

The tube thumped again, and the entrance erupted, spewing more flames and debris. The front double doors hung open.

Karga turned around and flashed a light at the Land Rover. The engine started, a cloud of dirt and chunks of grass flying as the vehicle raced to the hill.

NIKKI'S PISTOL CRASHED TWICE, and the guard closest to her dropped with a bloody crater on the side of his head.

The lights had gone out, the only illumination coming from the orange flame licking up the walls.

The curtains fueled the fire, and the room was now full of smoke. And screams. Screams of the wounded and panicked. Nobody was making a dash for the doors yet; the guests were combat vets who were waiting for the next bomb.

Nikki didn't wait. She holstered her pistol and grabbed the dead guard's SMG. She moved through the gloom, bumping into prostrate forms, gaining the doorway and slipping out.

In the open foyer, she considered options. Nobody emerged from any nearby rooms. She made for the basement steps and hurried down, the pitch-dark of the hallway unsurprising. She felt along the wall. Nikki stopped when she heard a man's voice.

"Can anybody hear me? Patrol, do you copy?"

A dim light glowed in the room—somebody with a flashlight. The door was open, and two people were standing while one slumped in a chair, gasping.

A woman's voice joined the man's.

"We can't wait, Ross."

Darien Foster.

Nikki rushed the doorway, the man swinging the flashlight her way as she zeroed in on Darien. The SMG chattered, the salvo cutting through

Darien with a series of wet slaps. Her short scream cut off as she toppled back. Nikki dropped to a squat, swinging the SMG to the man called Ross. He was digging for a holstered pistol when her next burst opened his stomach, his guts spilling onto the concrete floor. Her second salvo tore up his chest.

"Get the light!" Stiletto shouted.

His body protested as he pushed out of the chair, but Stiletto ignored the pain and took the flashlight from Nikki's hand.

The three slugs from the SMG had hit Darien high in the chest. Blood had pooled underneath her, and Scott couldn't avoid the puddle as he knelt beside her body and started feeling through her pockets.

"Should I have left her alive?" Nikki asked.

"Not with her pointing my own gun at me."

"What if she doesn't have the drive?"

"Then we go find somebody who does before whoever launched the bomb attack shows up."

Stiletto stood, but not before collecting the .45. "She doesn't have it. Come on."

"Check her bra."

"What?"

"Check her bra! I hide stuff there all the time."

Stiletto knelt again and pulled up Darien's shirt, feeling inside one cup, and then the other, and snatching the thumb drive from its hiding place.

"Good thinking." Stiletto shined the flash on the drive. It was undamaged.

Scott stowed it in a pocket and wiped his hands on his jeans. "Now we can go."

They stopped as automatic weapons sounding like buzz-saws echoed from the floor above.

Emil Karga snapped back the charging handle of his AK-104 as the Land Rover approached the castle.

The driver, to avoid the flaming cars, steered through the entry arch and stopped the vehicle in the center of the front lawn. Karga and his men piled out. The snipers had traded their rifles for AK-104s like Karga's, and the six men in combat black spread out as they trotted to the castle entrance. The heat of the fire warmed Karga's face. The place wasn't a fireball because of the stonework, but the materials burning inside produced much more smoke than he'd expected.

Karga stopped short as panicked guests started to emerge, braving the wrecked entrance for the fresh air beyond. Karga raised the AK-104 and pulled the trigger, his crew following, and the rapid automatic fire filled the night. The bodies of the guests littered what remained of the steps as the Russian gun crew filed inside.

More stragglers were frozen with fright in the foyer. One raised a gun, only to be quickly cut down by one of the Russians. Karga and Simokoff fired on the others, the guest's bodies turning to bloody ruin as the 7.62mm slugs ripped their limbs apart.

"Find the woman and kill her, then find the American and bring him to me," Karga ordered. His crew spread out, leaving him to explore on his own.

Presently, he found the steps to the basement.

STILETTO AND NIKKI were already moving down the hall, using the flashlight in occasional sweeps to see what lay ahead. Nikki gasped and gripped

Scott's arm, shoving him into the right-side wall. She froze against him.

Stiletto kept his mouth shut. She had heard something, and now he heard the sound too. Footsteps on the stairs. They were cautious, but not totally silent.

It has to be Karga, Stiletto thought. The bombs and the shooting. Who else would make the effort?

Stiletto urged Nikki forward, whispering for her to stay close to the wall.

There was a burst of gunfire behind them and Stiletto and Nikki hit the ground as the slugs bounced off the concrete, ricocheting back and forth with vicious whines.

As Nikki rose to resume moving down the hall once the last slug had finally stopped, Stiletto spun and let one round go from the .45. He aimed for where he thought the muzzle flash had come from, but his own ricochet confirmed a miss.

Stiletto stayed low as he moved forward, his left hand out in front of him. He moved slowly, his mind telling him to stop in the constant expectation of hitting a wall, but he ignored the instinct and continued through the total darkness of the hallway.

A latch clicked, and fresh air touched his face.

Side door ahead, the kind he'd envisioned Darien might have used for her own escape. When Stiletto eased through the door, Nikki waited on the other side with her weapon ready. Once Stiletto had passed her, she fired two shorts bursts, ricochets sounding again as Stiletto and Nikki started across the grass.

Smoke filled the still air, the heat from the fire palpable. They turned for the cars but stopped short. The vehicles were all smoldering wrecks. Useless.

Stiletto started to say something when automatic weapons fire kicked up the grass around them, geysers of dirt flying into the air. Nikki triggered the SMG as they ran for the creek behind the castle. There was only one gunner firing, but he'd call the rest of the crew.

At least now they could see a little in the light of the moon. Shouting behind them—the gunman calling for back-up. Gunfire popped, and the bullets zipped overhead.

The ground began to slope as they neared the creek and there was more shouting and more gunfire. "There are more of them!" Nikki shouted.

Stiletto didn't look back. His attention was on the trees ahead that served as the first barrier to the

creek. But then what? They were far from civilization. It wasn't a matter of getting to the nearest
town for help. They were in the middle of nowhere
with an enemy well equipped for chasing them
until he and Nikki dropped, and he was halfway
there, making demands on a damaged body that
would eventually turn on him.

The grass thinned as dirt and small rocks took
over, the slope steepening. Stiletto's left foot caught
on a tree root and sent him sprawling. He missed a
tree trunk as he landed, rolling down the slope to
where the ground met the water. The Colt left his
grip as he tumbled and he flailed for the gun, his
body coming to an abrupt stop when he splashed
into the cold creek.

"Scott!"

He heard Nikki's voice through the pounding
in his head as he sat up in a daze, his clothes wet
and a chill beginning to make him shiver. She slung
the SMG and helped him up.

"Are you hurt?"

"I've never been this banged up in my life,"
Scott stated. He moved with a slight limp, but a
check of his legs and ankles showed nothing
broken, and there was no time to look for the Colt
.45. The Russian gun crew appeared at the top of

the slope, and each man brought up his AK. Stiletto and Nikki scrambled for cover as the fusillade of gunfire rained down, the pair quickly diving into the thick of the forest beside the creek.

When the shooting stopped, Stiletto watched the Russians through a gap. They started down the slope. His kingdom for the Colt!

But Nikki still had some ammo in her SMG. She told Scott to plug his ears as she aimed through the branches and loosed two bursts. The SMG clicked empty, but the damage had been done. One of the Russians cried out and fell back and the others hurried, one tripping and the rest unable to avoid him. They all tumbled into the creek.

It might have been funny, but Stiletto wasn't laughing. He grabbed Nikki and they started moving again, staying where the forest was thickest but finding continuous obstacles with fallen trunks, entwined branches, and heavy undergrowth.

Karga's voice echoed as he shouted orders at his men as Stiletto and Nikki pressed ahead, stopping after another ten yards. They looked back. The gun crew was moving along the creek where there was mostly level ground, scanning the sloping foliage for their quarry. They were operating under the assumption that neither was without weapons, and Stiletto decided to help them along in that thinking. He located a rock about the size of a baseball, found an opening, and threw the rock as hard as he could. The rock sailed between the two gunners in front of the line and splashed in the water.

Scott urged Nikki up the slope, although that was easier said than done. His legs burned with pain, but he pushed on.

Karga yelled, "If you're reduced to throwing rocks like a peasant, you should surrender!"

Scott held back a long branch with a huge leaf for Nikki to climb under.

"We do not want you dead, Stiletto! There are people in Russia who will pay me well to hand you over alive."

Another couple of feet gained. Scott wanted to work his way back to the gunner Nikki had shot and take his equipment.

"You owe me a new deck of cards!"

Stiletto finally let out a laugh, a sharp rebuking look from Nikki his only reward.

He looked back. The Russians were now moving into the forest and starting up the slope. Their weapons wouldn't help them navigate very well, and that meant they'd climb slowly. He urged

Nikki on. Leaves and dried branches crumbled beneath them and branches snapped and poked, the sounds mixing with the racket the Russians made. A shot cracked, and Stiletto jumped. The bullet came nowhere near, only a gunman shooting at shadows.

Scott parted a pair of leaves and saw the prize ahead. The dead Russian lay on his face, arms and legs spread out. His AK-104 and web gear had gone untouched since his demise.

"Wait," Stiletto told Nikki, then, against his better instinct but confident that the Russians were well behind them, Stiletto broke through the foliage and scrambled to the dead man.

A shadow moved in front of him on the opposite side of the slope and Nikki screamed. Stiletto's hands were reaching for the AK-104 when the shadow became a gunman with fury in his eyes. He smashed the butt of his rifle into the side of Stiletto's face and he felt his body start to fall, but didn't feel it stop.

SIMOKOFF LET the American tumble as dirt and leaves bunched up beneath him and finally stopped the fall halfway to the creek.

He fired into the brush where the American had been. The woman was in there, and he had no orders to let her live.

Simokoff let off the trigger, yelling for his comrades, and approached the trees. He probed with his rifle, but there was no sign of the woman.

Presently the rest of his crew and Karga returned and stood over Stiletto's unconscious body.

"Where's the woman?" Karga asked.

"I don't know, but she can't have gotten far."

"We need to find her. *Now*."

The gun crew returned to the castle area, most of the fire out now, and spread out to search for Nikki, but like the smoke, she'd faded into the night.

Karga rallied the crew after nearly two hours. They couldn't stay any longer. He sent two men to collect Stiletto and their fallen comrade, then piled into the Land Rover and left the battle behind.

CHAPTER 15

Nikki figured she was a frightful mess.

Her clothes were blood-stained and filthy, her hair knotted and full of forest bits, but she stayed flat in the roadside ditch as far from the castle as she could get. When Karga's Land Rover finally departed, she stood and swiped uselessly at her outfit. At least the dirt disguised Darien's bloodstains.

The chilly night air dried the sweat on her face and neck, and her mind started calculating her next move without prompting.

Problem: Scott had been captured. He had the thumb drive.

Problem: Who the hell was the Russian guy, and where would they take Scott?

Solution: Paris. Suzi.

Problem: How to get there?

She needed a telephone. She started walking along the road, her own aches and pains minor to what Scott must be feeling. She'd walk all night if she had to. Eventually, she'd either pass out on the pavement or flag down a vehicle.

The latter happened within three hours.

A car came around a bend, the headlamps hit Nikki dead on, and the driver braked. A woman jumped out from the passenger side and ran to her, and she mumbled a story about a boyfriend beating her and tossing her from his truck. The woman and the man driving didn't need more than that to put her in the back seat and take her to their country home.

Nikki slept through the night but refused the couple's offer of further help. She only wanted a ride to the nearest town, where she'd call somebody to come and get her.

Nikki sat on a park bench on a moderately busy street. She had not taken the time to learn the town's name, but it was busy enough that nobody eavesdropped on her conversation. She bought a pre-paid cell phone from an electronics store to call Suzi. She was wearing borrowed clothes given to her by the wife of the couple who had picked her up. They were half a size too big, but a belt helped keep the jeans up and she rolled the sleeves of the blouse so the cuffs didn't cover her hands.

She dialed Suzi and waited for her to pick up.

"WHY ARE you calling instead of Scott?" Suzi asked. She still occupied the Paris suite overlooking the Eiffel Tower.

"Long story, but some Russian guy has Scott, and I need to find him."

"What do you mean, *some Russian guy?*"

"Goddammit, Suzi, somebody who says Scott owes him a deck of cards."

"Must be Karga." Suzi wheeled from her spot in front of the television to the dining table where her computer sat at the ready. Her fingers flew across the keys as she told Nikki of Scott's vendetta with Emil Karga.

"He operates out of the Balkans, but I'm not sure exactly where," Suzi explained. "I can tell you that he has a partner named Dimitri Yorsin. Apply a little pressure, and he should talk."

"I need help."

Suzi opened her email and started typing

addresses. "I'm already contacting a pair of mercs Scott worked with recently. They go by the names Hardball and Short Fuse. How much do you want to spend?"

"Whatever it takes," Nikki told her.

"Where are you?"

"Ireland." Nikki explained about the couple who found her.

"I'll look up the closest airport and get a charter for you. Call me on the way and I'll give you more on Yorsin."

Somewhere in Serbia

NIKKI FORTUNE, wearing new clothes that fit and with her hair tied back, entered the Federal Association of Globe Trotters and thought the pub's name was appropriate considering the last several days. She'd never traveled so much in her life.

The interior was brightly lit, its wood walls and floor smartly polished and decorated with various pieces of memorabilia from around the world. Nikki wove through the full tables and dodged the rushing waitstaff, the place loud with conversation and kitchen noise. She pulled out an empty chair at a rear corner table and joined the two men already seated.

She shook hands with Hardball and Short Fuse.

"I hear we're going door-busting," the stocky Short Fuse said.

"Right, but we need to find Karga's partner and make him talk first."

The pub was in the heart of downtown Belgrade, and not all of the patrons were there for a night out. The Belgrade underground was a hub of illegal trafficking, and a lot of business was being done at the surrounding tables.

A waitress came over, and Nikki ordered a beer. When the frosty mug arrived, she took a long drink.

"Look over your left shoulder," Hardball said. "Table by the wall."

She covered her glance by admiring the wall decorations.

The man to whom Hardball referred was middle-aged and dark-haired, wearing a black shirt and matching slacks. Even his shoes were black, albeit with silver tips on the laces.

Dimitri Yorsin. His face matched the picture Suzi had sent during Nikki's charter flight.

Yorsin sat across from a young brunette with her hair curled down her back and her legs crossed, one high-heeled shoe dangling off her right foot. They had drinks and a plate of appetizers on the table.

"Where's he live?" Nikki asked, swallowing more beer.

"High-rise condo not too far away," Short Fuse told her.

A WAITRESS BOXED the left-over appetizers and handed the box to Yorsin as he and the brunette departed. He kissed her good-bye before putting her in a cab and climbed into a Mercedes parked on the street.

Nikki, Short Fuse, and Hardball followed the Mercedes. Hardball drove. He said he knew the streets well from previous jobs in the area. Nikki didn't ask for details.

DIMITRI YORSIN PUT down the phone and unlocked the door. Back on the couch, he watched more of the football game on the television, the camera on the goalie, who had blocked a shot that should have been dead-on.

Yorsin had been a football fan from his youth and had a set of signed photos of the local team hanging beside the door of his high-rise condo. The place was clean, but the furniture was mismatched here and there. Yorsin cared more for comfort than aesthetics.

Still dressed in his black shirt, slacks, and shoes, Yorsin wasn't expecting any trouble.

The door opened and Anatoly, one of the collectors for Yorsin's loansharking operation, entered. He carried a bulging leather pouch.

Yorsin stood to shake hands, and they moved to the adjoining kitchen. Anatoly declined a beer, opened the pouch, and shook out cash onto the counter.

"Very nice," Yorsin said. "Any trouble?"

"Not today," Anatoly replied. "I didn't have to take out Big Bertha." He patted the holstered .44 Magnum revolver under his arm.

Yorsin collected the money into two stacks.

"Probably for the best," he said. "With what Karga is up to, we don't need the attention."

Anatoly stiffed. "Who the hell is that?"

As Yorsin turned to the patio doors indicated

by Anatoly's gaze, a woman on the other side of the glass picked up a chair and threw it. The chair shattered the panes, bits of glass flying inside and spreading across the carpet.

The woman stepped inside with an automatic in her right hand.

Anatoly clawed for Big Bertha and started to raise the stainless .44 Magnum, which was the last thing he ever did.

Nikki Fortune and Short Fuse ran across the roof and secured a rope to an exposed pipe. Tossing the rest over the side, she looked down at Yorsin's balcony. She told Short Fuse to follow her after she broke the windows and rappelled over the edge. When she reached the balcony, Yorsin stood with his back to the patio, but the other man with him noticed her right away.

Nikki picked up a metal chair and launched it through the patio doors, then went inside with a Beretta 92FS in hand. When the other man drew a stainless revolver, Nikki fired twice in quick succession.

Anatoly crashed against the refrigerator and left a smear of blood on the tile floor when he hit it.

His beloved Big Bertha flew from his grip and hit the wall with a thud.

Nikki swung the Beretta on Yorsin as Short Fuse's feet touched the patio behind her. The stocky bomb expert entered with an HK UMP9 zeroed on Yorsin.

The color faded from Yorsin's face and he bolted around the counter, slipping on Anatoly's blood. He fell ass-first on the floor and scrambled toward Big Bertha, but Nikki reached him first, casually walking over to kick Yorsin in the ribs.

Yorsin yelled and lunged for the revolver again, so Nikki kicked him again. This time the fire left Yorsin and he lay flat, wheezing. Nikki picked up the revolver. Stainless Smith & Wesson Model 629 —nice piece. Nikki stuck it in her belt. She also holstered the Beretta.

Short Fuse slung his SMG and helped her drag Yorsin to the couch, where they propped him upright. Nikki found the remote and turned off the television.

The home team was losing anyway.

NIKKI SLAPPED Yorsin out of his daze.

The Russian gripped his ribs with both hands.

"Emil Karga," Nikki began. "Where is he?"

"Go to hell."

Nikki snapped her fingers, and Short Fuse slammed the butt of his HK into Yorsin's midsection.

Yorsin winced, biting off a scream, and inhaled sharply. "You won't get anywhere *beating* me."

Nikki folded her arms. "You might have a point. Short Fuse?"

"Yes?"

"Let's dangle him over the balcony."

"Hold my weapon."

Nikki took the HK as Short Fuse grabbed Yorsin's shirt. He hauled him off the couch and over his shoulder and started for the patio, bits of glass crunching under his feet. Yorsin yelled and struggled, but Short Fuse held him tight.

The Russian yelled some more as Short Fuse lifted him off his shoulders and let him dangle over the railing, holding Yorsin's legs in a bear hug. Yorsin extended his arms as if that would stop him from falling, any screams now caught in his throat as the street beckoned below.

Nikki stood beside Short Fuse, who was now sweating from the strain of holding onto Yorsin.

"Hurry," Short Fuse urged.

Yorsin yelled.

Nikki leaned over the rail. "Change your mind?"

"Okay! Okay!"

"Where's Karga?"

"In the hills south of the city! Off the E-75!"

"What's the address?"

Yorsin told her the house number.

"Very good, Dimitri."

"Let me up!"

"And leave you alive to call him?" Nikki snapped her fingers.

Yorsin yelled as Short Fuse released his grip.

Gravity took over, and the wind swallowed Yorsin's scream.

HARDBALL STARTED THE CAR. "That might be a little tough to clean up."

Nikki and Short Fuse buckled their seatbelts as Hardball swung out of the parking lot.

"Forget it," she said. "His football team lost, and he got depressed."

Short Fuse laughed. "Works for me."

"Let's go get Scott," Nikki said.

· · ·

Nikki, Hardball, and Short Fuse, their faces now streaked with black cosmetics, carried weapons from the trunk of the car as they moved over the soft ground through the thin forest.

Mud caked their boots. Branches yielded without snapping. As they neared Karga's cabin, Hardball raised his right arm to signal the others to stop and drop.

Nikki scooted on her belly to the edge of the cabin's dirt-and-bark yard. The one-story cabin with a wraparound porch would have been a nice retreat had it not been the domicile of an international criminal.

No troops on patrol. Lights burned inside. Good sign.

"What do you think?" Nikki asked.

Hardball said, "I'd like to get a little closer before we start shooting in case we got the wrong place."

"Okay." Nikki worried that if Hardball was right, they had no other leads. Yorsin had to have been telling the truth. She hoped.

Nikki broke cover first, followed by Short Fuse. Hardball rose from a few feet behind and took two steps forward, passing between a pair of trees. His right boot caught on something, and a pop echoed.

Before he could yell a warning, the blast from the trip-wired grenade cut into him and his brief scream filled the night.

Short Fuse looked back at Hardball's shattered body, his mouth open in shock.

Nikki shouted, "Take cover!" as a shooter started firing from the wraparound deck.

CHAPTER 16

SCOTT WOKE up in a plush tan leather chair. His hands were tied in front of him. His head throbbed where the rifle stock had impacted, and the spot felt wet to the touch. He wiped the little spots of blood on his shirt.

The only sound besides the pounding in his head was the drone of a jet engine, and he raised his head. Another Lear Jet. The cabin was narrower but had the usual amenities.

Stiletto looked down. His clothes were muddy, torn, and sweat-stained, and he smelled awful. Worse, his belt was gone.

"I figured you deserved a tiny bit of comfort, so we didn't tie your hands behind your back."

Emil Karga sat across from him with a solitaire layout on the table between them.

"You don't have to thank me."

"I wasn't going to," Stiletto said.

Karga didn't look up. He placed cards carefully.

"I wondered how you got free when we had you in the trunk," Karga said, "and your belt answered my question. So that's gone too."

"That's okay, it's time I learned some new tricks."

Karga placed another card in the line-up. "I play solitaire to relax my mind," the Russian said. "I often need the distraction from business. When you so brutally tossed away my other deck, you dealt me a bigger blow than you realized."

"Pun intended?"

"Hmm?" Karga looked up. "Oh, you made a funny. I suppose you do the same with your sketch pad. What would you have done if I threw that away?"

"Buy another? It's not like they're rare or anything."

Karga returned to his game, searching in vain for a spot for the six of diamonds before discarding it.

"You're worth almost half a million US dollars to Moscow, did you know this?"

"I had no idea."

"You're wanted for illegally entering the country and blowing up a power station. Is that why you were fired from the CIA?"

"Probably."

Karga played another card.

"You met Mr. Simokoff, poor Killkin's replacement."

Scott looked at the man seated on the opposite side of the cabin's aisle. He still cradled his AK-104.

"I'm glad your name isn't as funny as the other guy's."

Simokoff showed no reaction.

"Are we going straight to Moscow?" Stiletto asked.

"No, Belgrade. I have to finish my business with the Jordan Corp. data, and then you will be collected."

"Always figured that was where your home base was."

"Yet you never tried very hard to find me." Karga raised his head again. "Why is that? You'd sworn vengeance for the two agents I killed when you tried to apprehend me, but you didn't do anything about that in the last three years. How come?"

"Too busy, I guess."

"Or you wanted a carrot."

"I'm not a vegetable guy."

"That's not what I mean. You needed a reason for being. Something to motivate yourself. If I was gone, how would you justify your life?"

"You're thinking too hard, Emil."

"Am I?"

"I'm motivated by many things."

"Of course you are."

"I've been doing this for a lot longer than three years, Emil. Who was the carrot before you?"

"Only you can answer that," Karga told him.

Stiletto already knew the answer.

He lived to fight men like Karga because he could, and somebody had to. There were a lot of men like Scott, and too many like Karga. And when the time came, Scott would deal with Karga the same way he'd dealt with the others. Coldly. Efficiently. No wasted bullets.

But there was another answer, too—the one Scott didn't like to talk about. He was running. From himself. From the past. From his failures as a husband and a father. But he had no intention of telling Karga any of that.

It was hard enough admitting it to himself.

THE JET LANDED IN BELGRADE, where the overcast hung above the private hanger as a pair of SUVs pulled up.

Karga and Simokoff rode in the first SUV with Scott jammed between them in the back seat. The rest of the gun crew rode in the other SUV.

Stiletto watched Belgrade flash by as they traveled from the Nikola Tesla Airport and merged from the E-70 freeway to the E-75. Stiletto caught a whiff of the odor that emanated from him; unlike the two beside him, he had not had the luxury of using the jet's shower. He hoped his stink annoyed them. The two vehicles remained on the E-75 for a while, finally pulling off an exit outside the city. Stiletto lost mental track of their direction as the driver made a series of turns and double-backs to see if they were being followed. Stiletto laughed.

"What's funny?" Karga said.

"If you're afraid my people are behind us, relax. The woman I was with has no idea what your name is."

"She left you behind, you know. We tried to find her but had no luck."

"I figured she'd do something like that."

"She's not the woman of virtue you Americans highly prize?"

"I think she was only using me to get the Jordan Corp. data."

Karga chuckled. "You both failed."

"She was great in the sack, though. I'm not much of a virtue guy."

"I hope she was the best lay of your life because she's also your last."

Stiletto didn't respond.

The SUVs came to a stop on a dirt driveway in front of a single-level cabin with a wraparound porch. Karga exited first, Simokoff covering Stiletto with an automatic. He held Scott in the SUV until the rest of the team was out of the second vehicle, standing by with ready weapons, then prodded Stiletto out of the back seat.

The inside of the cabin looked nice, lots of soft colors, but Stiletto had no time to admire the interior design effort. Simokoff kept possession of him and steered Scott down a hallway to an empty room. Simokoff shoved, and Scott tumbled to the floor.

"You'll be fed if you behave," Simokoff said.

"I think that's the first time I've heard you speak," Stiletto stated. He rose to his knees as Simokoff shut and locked the door.

At least the room was quiet, but the only window was barred from the outside, and there was no furniture, but the carpet was relatively soft. Scott moved his wrists; the binding was tight and he didn't have his belt, so there'd be no razor trick this time. Scott stretched out in a corner and decided to give his body a rest while his mind worked out an escape plan.

"HOLDING HIM HERE IS DANGEROUS," Simokoff argued.

Karga stood in the kitchen scooping grounds into a coffee maker. He did not reply.

"Trading him to Moscow invites trouble we don't need."

Karga poured in water and pressed the Brew button. He said, "We won't be here long enough for him to make a plan."

Simokoff took a deep breath.

"Create a schedule for the men and get some rest," Karga ordered.

Simokoff left the kitchen as the scent of French roast filled the room.

STILETTO AWOKE to sun streaming through the barred window, the beam highlighting the dust in the air. His body was stiff and sore, so he stood and began a series of stretches and exercises to work out the kinks. His head still hurt, but the welt had stopped bleeding. Now it was a lump. He felt dizzy and sat down—probably a concussion. Not his first.

An armed trooper with a scowl escorted him to the bathroom, where he removed the rope from Stiletto's wrists so he could splash water on his face and use the toilet. The trooper remained in the doorway, but only one, who held his AK at the ready. It wouldn't take much to throw water in the man's face as a distraction and try for the rifle if he got close enough, but Scott wanted to bide his time and see what other chances developed. The trooper today would be ready. Tomorrow? Maybe not. But did he have that much time?

Back in the room with the door locked once again, his hands now free, Stiletto stretched out on the floor and shut his eyes. His vision was spinning, and he was truly in no shape to fight. But he also wasn't going to Russia.

One way or another he would get away, even if it meant leaving Karga alive for another round sometime in the future.

CRICKETS CHIRPED. Simokoff, on night watch, walked the length of the wraparound porch, enjoying the cool night air and especially the solitude. He'd scheduled himself for this shift because he didn't get much alone-time in his line of work.

He hadn't been happy about keeping the American two days ago, but now Karga had made up his mind. The buyers for the Jordan Corp. data would arrive within the next twelve hours, so at least they'd be moving on soon, if not as soon as Simokoff would have preferred.

Karga had at least consented to let him lay booby traps around the perimeter, jury-rigged as they were with grenades instead of proper and more suitable explosives. They would do the job if Stiletto had any friends able to track them.

Emil Karga, like many of his ilk who had escaped capture for so long, had become complacent.

At least in Simokoff's opinion.

He walked along one side of the house to where the deck ended at the rear, turned and started for the front again, wishing he hadn't quit smoking. It was often the best way to pass the time while on night watch.

Simokoff had reached the front of the house when one of his trip-wired grenades exploded and filled the dark night with a brilliant flash of flame.

He started shouting for backup as he braced on the deck rail and opened fire. Two other troopers quickly joined him, dropping to one knee and following his example. The rest of the gun crew arrived and lined up along the rail. The shock-waves generated by the cracking Kalashnikov rifles brushed past Simokoff's face.

Simokoff lifted his finger off the trigger as he scanned the tree line, where two figures moved. He sighted on one and fired again. Return salvos smacked the wall behind him, shattering a window.

Simokoff stayed low and slipped back inside as his crew continued firing. A burst of rounds splintered the doorway, but he ignored the shrapnel and kept going.

. . .

STILETTO TRIED to see if there was any way to signal the raiding party from his window, but there was no activity on his side of the house.

His pulse raced and he was fully alert, pain forgotten. Somebody had found him. Nikki?

The door crashed open, and Simokoff leveled the AK.

"If your friends are so interested in saving you, maybe they'll have second thoughts if they might accidentally kill you." The Russian started forward. "Turn around. You'll be a perfect human shield."

"You should have killed me when you had the chance," Scott suggested.

He lunged for the AK, clamping one hand on the forward stock and using his free left elbow to smash Simokoff's nose, feeling it crack under the impact. The Russian didn't fall, so Stiletto shoved the AK up and back, cracking Simokoff's trigger finger, and that made him choke and scream at the same time. He shoved Simokoff out into the hall, wrenching the AK-104 from his useless right hand, and brought the rifle to his shoulder. Simokoff hit the opposite wall, and Stiletto pinned him there with a spray from the AK. Pieces of Simokoff's upper body splattered all over the hall, and his body slid down the wall into a sitting position on the floor.

Stiletto, gasping, leaned against the doorway a moment as his vision tilted left. Concussion or not, he had to finish the fight and get back home, wherever that happened to be. Stripping Simokoff of his spare ammo and pistol, Stiletto ran toward the sound of continuous gunfire.

Nikki cursed when she saw her burst miss the guy going back inside, but there was no time to dwell on that. The other four shooters kept her busy. She fired and moved, fired and moved, staying flat and rolling left or right after each salvo. Short Fuse, back in the trees, did the same, but the small targets were hard to hit.

Then somebody exited the house and Nikki held her fire.

Stiletto! The troopers on the deck didn't take notice as Scott started shooting, hosing the gun crew. Nikki ran for the deck and caught Short Fuse in her peripheral vision. Stiletto moved forward, continuing to blast the gun crew from behind until their insides were leaking through the gaps in the deck planks.

"What kept you?" Scott asked as she and Short Fuse leaped under the railing.

Nikki started to answer when Karga appeared at the end of the room inside the cabin and fired a pistol. She twisted right and started to drop, feeling the heat of the passing bullet as it singed her nose.

CHAPTER 17

STILETTO PIVOTED with the AK at his hip.

He didn't give Karga another chance to shoot. The AK kicked and flame licked from the barrel, Karga screaming as the rounds ripped apart his flesh and reduced him to bloody hamburger from stomach to neck. Karga fell hard on his back.

Scott tossed the empty AK and took out Simokoff's pistol, a nine-millimeter Glock, crossed to Karga's body, and put two more rounds through his head. Kneeling beside the body, he quickly rummaged through the man's pockets, finding the thumb drive in a back pocket. He dropped it into one of his own pockets and raced back to Nikki and Short Fuse.

They were getting up from where they'd dropped. He helped Nikki to her feet and slapped Short Fuse on the shoulder.

"Where's Hardball?"

Nikki looked away and Short Fuse shook his head.

"The explosion?" Scott asked.

"He didn't make it," Short Fuse said.

Stiletto blinked a few times.

"We gotta go," Nikki urged.

"Yeah," Stiletto told her.

With Short Fuse behind the wheel, Nikki beside him, and Scott in back, they left the cabin and Hardball's body behind.

Scott hated the idea of leaving a man behind. It was not the way it was done in the "old" world, where there had been codes and understandings that meant something. Now guys only showed up if you paid, and if you got killed, your body remained where you fell. This was the "new" world, and Scott needed to get used to it. Hardball would have understood and expected nothing less. The job came first, then the getaway. Losing more men to recover bodies wasn't part of the plan. It wasn't what they were paid for.

Neither Short Fuse nor Nikki spoke as the car continued on, and that was fine. Stiletto wanted to think.

He fingered the thumb drive and thought of what he'd promised Kim Jordan. How many weeks had passed? The new world didn't have to be entirely cold-blooded. There could still be codes and understandings that meant something. Let the rest of them, Stiletto decided, get used to *his* way of finishing a job.

NIKKI'S CONTACTS proved invaluable once again, providing transportation by car out of Belgrade south to Leskovac where the Belgrade authorities wouldn't be searching for foreigners who might have been involved in a gun battle at a certain cabin and looked the part. It was a long drive, three hours, but a private jet waited at the end of the journey.

Stiletto was getting sick of private jets. He suddenly wanted the cramped compartment of an economy-class cabin and a bag of peanuts.

Short Fuse made alternate plans once they reached Leskovac and left them at Mira Airport.

Once the jet had climbed through the cloud layer, Stiletto took a hot shower in a too small bathroom in the back of the plane. It sure felt good, regardless of how many times he banged his elbows.

He had to put his dirty clothes back on afterward, but he felt worlds better, and Nikki had a Maker's and Coke waiting for him when he returned to the passenger cabin. He eased into a soft leather seat, and the leather let out a hiss as his body sank into the cushions.

Nikki sat in the chair beside him.

"My father will be glad Darien is dead," she said.

"What a waste." Scott swallowed some of his drink.

"What do you mean?"

"She was a murderer and a criminal and deserved what she got, but I can't help being a little sympathetic toward her for wanting to avenge her parents. Too bad she chose the wrong path."

"What other avenue was there?"

"If she'd joined our side, she might have been a great asset."

Nikki frowned. "I don't normally meet a man so philosophical."

"I'm full of surprises."

She smiled and sipped her wine. Stiletto felt the left pocket of his wrecked trousers. The thumb drive was still there. He took it out and examined it. Specks of dried blood covered one side. She hadn't switched it with another while he was showering.

He looked at her and was surprised to see her already looking at him. Their eyes met.

"I wasn't after that," Nikki told him.

"I know."

He'd been wrong about her, and he was glad.

He took another drink and let his mind wander to another thought, this one a little more disturbing.

The Russians had a price on his head.

Half a million, Karga had said.

Stiletto didn't know what to do with the information yet, but at some point, he'd need to pay attention and see if there was a way to resolve the issue without surrendering. Or perhaps he'd need to send the Russians a message that communicated clearly that he wasn't going to play their games.

. . .

THE JET LANDED IN SICILY, and Stiletto remained with Nikki and her father long enough to get some rest, see a doctor, and let his body heal. After a couple of weeks, he made arrangements to fly back to Seattle.

Nikki and her father rode with Scott to the airport, where the old man handed him a pair of Cuban Cohibas and promised to provide help if Stiletto ever needed it. Nikki's wink promised much more.

He landed at SeaTac once more and rented a car to drive to Jordan Corp. The building seemed to be humming right along as he entered the lobby, the security guard with the ill-fitting suit still behind the front desk.

On one wall near the desk, the company had placed a memorial to Elias Campbell and the security guards killed by Darien Foster. Stiletto paused before it for a moment before the guard said, "Ms. Jordan isn't here right now, sir."

Scott said that was okay. He knew where to find her.

He grinned at the usual tinge of moisture in the air as he walked the three blocks to the coffee shop where he and Kim had forged more than a business relationship.

He stopped in front of the large-paned window. She sat behind it, alone at a small table, looking out at the world as it passed her by.

When their eyes met, Stiletto raised a hand in a casual wave. Then he went inside and joined her.

A LOOK AT: THE MINAS
DECEPTION (A SCOTT STILETTO
THRILLER 5)
BY BRIAN DRAKE

TYRANNY MUST BE VANQUISHED

VENEZUELA IS in the midst of a civil war. Rebel
forces are facing the hardened army of dictator
Lazaro Minas, who uses death squads and secret
prisons to keep dissent against his regime to a mini-
mum. Hostilities have ceased after a hurricane
ravages the island, but tempers are short, and both
sides are itching to resume the fight.

Scott Stiletto's mission is to bring guns and
medical supplies to the rebels, and the horror of
what they're facing propels him into the fight. This
is a battle he cannot ignore. The innocent suffer
while under the boot of a dictator who presents

himself to the world as a benign leader equal to others.

Venezuela is a powder keg where madmen control others with fear and violence. Scott Stiletto plans to show them what real fear – and sudden death – feels like.

Full of nail-biting suspense – The Minas Deception is the fifth book in the hard-edged Scott Stiletto series.

AVAILABLE JULY 2019 FROM BRIAN DRAKE AND WOLFPACK PUBLISHING

A twenty-five year veteran of radio and television broadcasting, Brian Drake has spent his career in San Francisco where he's filled writing, producing, and reporting duties with stations such as KPIX-TV, KCBS, KQED, among many others. Currently carrying out sports and traffic reporting duties for Bloomberg 960, Brian Drake spends time between reports and carefully guarded morning and evening hours cranking out action/adventure tales. A love of reading when he was younger inspired him to create his own stories, and he sold his first short story, "The Desperate Minutes," to an obscure webzine when he was 25 (more years ago than he cares to remember, so don't ask). Many more short story sales followed before he expanded to novels, entering the self-publishing field in 2010, and quickly building enough of a following to attract the attention of several publishers and other writing professionals. Brian Drake lives in California with his wife and two cats, and when he's not writing he is usually blasting along the back roads in his Corvette with his wife telling him not to drive so fast, but the engine is so loud he usually can't hear her.

You will find him regularly blogging at
www.briandrake88.blogspot.com

Find more great titles by Brian Drake and Wolfpack Publishing, here:
https://wolfpackpublishing.com/brian-drake/

Made in the USA
Middletown, DE
16 July 2019